He should  her.

Now where did that leave him? With a yearning for more and a woman who would hate him.

He should have stayed, should have reassured her, should have at least had the decency to admit the whole thing as his fault before he had walked out.

But she had thrown him with her pale elegance and honesty and with the fumbled bank notes pushed uncertainly at him.

To even think that she would pay him?

Absolute incredulity replaced irritation, and that in turn was replaced by something…more akin to respect.

She was the one all others aspired to be like, the pinnacle of manners and deportment and it cannot have been easy for her to have even asked what she did.

* * *

Mistletoe Magic
Harlequin® Historical #973—December 2009

MISTLETOE MAGIC
Sophia James

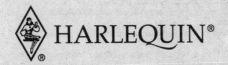

HARLEQUIN®

TORONTO • NEW YORK • LONDON
AMSTERDAM • PARIS • SYDNEY • HAMBURG
STOCKHOLM • ATHENS • TOKYO • MILAN • MADRID
PRAGUE • WARSAW • BUDAPEST • AUCKLAND

Recycling programs
for this product may
not exist in your area.

ISBN-13: 978-0-373-29573-9

MISTLETOE MAGIC

Copyright © 2009 by Sophia James.

First North American Publication 2009.

This edition published by arrangement with Harlequin Books S.A.

® and TM are trademarks of the publisher. Trademarks indicated with
® are registered in the United States Patent and Trademark Office, the
Canadian Trade Marks Office and in other countries.

www.eHarlequin.com

Printed in U.S.A.

Author Note

Christmas is a time of family and laughter and joyousness, a time when all the good things in the world seem to come together in a crescendo of happiness.

But what happens when people have no family left or the secrets that bind them to their kin preclude the simple ability to embrace the haphazard chaos that is often Christmas?

In this story I wanted to draw in two people on the edge of loneliness and add children, pets, color and carols. I wanted to see whether the magic of the season had its own power and whether a kiss bought under a sprig of mistletoe could change two lives forever.

I'd like to dedicate this book to my friend Jane, whose sense of style inspired Lillian.

Prologue

Lucas Clairmont found the letter by chance, wrapped in velvet and hidden in the space beneath the font in the Clairmont family chapel.

A love letter to his wife from a man he had little knowledge of and coined in a language that had him reaching for the pew behind him and sitting down.

Heavily.

He knew their marriage had been, at best, an unexceptional union, but it was the betrayal in the last few lines of the missive that was unexpected. His uncle's land was mentioned in connection with the Baltimore Gaslight Company's intention of developing their lines. Luc shook his head—he knew Stuart Clairmont had had no notion of such a scheme and the land, bought cheaply by Elizabeth's lover, had been sold for a fortune only a few months later.

Loss and guilt punctuated the harder emotion of anger. Jesus! Stuart had died a broken man and a vengeful one.

'Find the bastard, Luc,' he had uttered in the last few hours of his life, 'and kill him.'

At the time Luc had thought the command extreme, but now with the evidence of another truth in hand…

Screwing up the parchment, he let it slip through his fingers on to the cold stone floor, the written words still teasing him, even from a distance.

His marriage had been as much of a sham as his childhood, all show and no substance, but the love of his uncle had never wavered.

Shaking his head, he felt the sharp stab of sobriety, the taste of last night's whisky and the few bought hours of oblivion paid for dearly this morning, as his demons whispered vengeance.

Here in the chapel though, there lay the sort of silence that only God's dwelling could offer with the light streaming in through the stained glass window.

Jesus on the cross!

Luc's fingers squeezed against the hard smooth wood of oak benches, thinking that his own crown of thorns was far less visible.

'Lord, help me,' he enunciated, catching sight of the pale blue eyes of a painted cupid, hair a strange shade of silver blonde, and white clothes falling in folds on to the skin of a nearby sinner, dazzling him with light.

A sinner just like him, Luc thought, as the last effects of moonshine wore off and a headache he'd have until tomorrow started to pound.

Elizabeth. His wife.

He'd been away too much to be the sort of husband he should have been, but the truth of her liaison was as unexpected as her death six months ago. His thoughts of grief unravelled into a sort of bone-hard wrath that shocked him. Deceit and lies were written into every word of these outpourings.

He should not care. He should consign the evidence of his wife's infidelity to a fire, but he found that he couldn't because a certain truth was percolating.

Revenge! One of the seven deadly sins. Today, however, it was not so damning and the ennui that had consumed him lifted slightly.

It would mean going back to England. Again.

His home once.

Perhaps he could claim it back for a while, for apart from the land there was nothing left to hold him here. Besides, Hawk and Nathaniel had asked him to come back to London repeatedly, and he felt a sudden need for the company of his two closest friends.

'Ahhh, Stuart,' he whispered the name and liked the echo of it. The bastard who had swindled his uncle was in London, living on the profit of his ill-gotten gains no doubt.

Daniel Davenport. The name was engraved in his mind like a brand, seared into flesh.

But to kill him? The dying glances of others he had consigned to the hereafter rose from memory.

Not again! He leaned back on the pew and breathed in, trying to determine only the exact amount of force necessary to make Elizabeth's lover sorry.

Chapter One

London—November 1853

'Miss Davenport is a young woman any mother would be proud of, would you not say, Sybil?'

'Indeed, I would, for she countenances no scandal whatsoever. A reputation unsullied in each corner of her life, and a paragon of good sense, good taste and good comportment.'

Lillian Davenport listened to the compliments from her place in the little room, deciding that the two older women hadn't a notion of her being there. To alert them of her overhearing such a private matter would now cause them only embarrassment and so she stayed silent, letting the heavy petticoats in her hands fall to her side and ironing out the creases in white shot silk with her fingers.

'If only my Jane had the sort of grace that she has, I

often say to Gerald. If only we had drilled in the importance of the social codes as Ernest Davenport did, we
might have been blessed with a very different daughter.'

'Sometimes I think you are too hard on your girl,
Sybil. She has her own virtue after all and…'

They were moving away now and out of the ladies'
retiring room. Lillian heard the door close and tilted her
head, the last of the sentence lost into nothingness.

One minute. She would give them that before she
opened the door and took her leave.

*A paragon of good sense, good taste and good
comportment.*

A smile began to form on her face, though she
squashed it down. Pride was a sin in its own right and
she had no desire to be thought of as boastful.

Still…it was hard not to be pleased with such unexpected praise and, although she frequently detected a
general commendation on her manners, it was not often
that the words were so direct or honest.

Washing her hands, she shook off the excess, noting
how the white gold in her new birthday bracelet caught
the light from above. Twenty-five yesterday. Her euphoria
died a little, though she pushed the unsettled feeling down
as she walked out into a salon of the Lenningtons' townhouse and straight into some sort of fight.

'I think you cheated, you blackguard.' Her cousin
Daniel's tones were hardly civil and came from a very
close quarter.

'Then call me out. I am equally at home with

swords or pistols.' Another voice. Laconic. The drawl
of a man new from the former colonies, the laughter
in it unexpected.

'And have you kill me?'

'Life or death, Lord Davenport, take your choice or
stop your whining.'

There was the sound of pushing and shoving and the
two assailants came suddenly into view, Daniel's head
now locked in the bent elbow of a tall, dark-haired man,
her cousin's eyes bulging from the pressure and his fair
hair plastered wet across his forehead.

Lillian was speechless as her glance drew upwards
into the face of the assailant. Jacket unbuttoned and
with cravat askew, the stranger's jaw was heavily
shadowed by dark stubble and she was transfixed by two
golden eyes brushed in humour that stared now straight
at her. Unrepentant. Unapologetic. Pure and raw man
with blood on his lip and danger imprinted in every line
of his body.

It seemed that her own throat choked with the contact,
her heart slamming full into the ribs of her breast in one
heavy blow, leaving her with no breath. A warmth that
she had never before felt slid easily from her stomach,
fusing even the tips of her fingers with heat, and with it
came some other nameless thing, echoing on the edge
of a knowledge as old as time. Shocking. Dreadful. She
pulled her eyes from his and turned on her heels, but not
before she had seen him tip his head at her, the wink he
delivered licentious and untrammelled.

Mannerless, she decided, and American, and with more than a dozen other men and women looking on she knew the gossip about the fight would spread with an unstoppable haste.

Pulling the door to the retiring room open again, she returned to the same place she had left not more than a few minutes prior.

Anger consumed her.

And dread.

Who was he? She held out one hand and watched it shake before laying it down on her lap and shutting her eyes. A headache had begun to form and behind the pain came a wilder and more unwieldy longing.

'Stop it,' she whispered to herself, placing cold fingers across her lips to soften the sound as the door opened and other women came in, giggling this time and young.

'I love these balls. I love the music and the colour and the gowns…'

'And of all the gowns I love Lillian Davenport's best. Where does she get her clothes from, I wonder? Ester Hamilton says from London, but I would wager France—a modiste from Paris, perhaps, and a milliner from Florence? With all her money she could have them brought from anywhere.'

'Did you see her exquisite bracelet? Her father gave it to her for her birthday. Her twenty-fifth birthday!'

'Twenty-five! Poor Lillian,' the other espoused, 'and no husband or children either! My God, if she does not find a groom soon…'

'Oh, I would not go that far, Harriet. Some women like to live alone.'

'No woman wants to live alone, you peagoose. Besides Lord Wilcox-Rice has been paying her a lot of attention tonight. Perhaps she will fall in love with him and have the wedding of the year in the spring.'

The other girl tittered as they departed, leaving Lillian speechless.

Poor Lillian!

Poor Lillian?

Paragon to poor in all of five minutes, and a stranger outside who made her heart beat in a way that worried her.

'Mama?' The sound came in a prayer. 'Please, Lord, do not let me be anything like Mama.' She pushed the thought away. She would not see this colonial ruffian again; furthermore, if his behaviour tonight was anything to go by, she doubted he would be invited into any house of repute in the future. The thought relaxed her—after all, they were the only sort of homes that she frequented!

Wiping her brow, she stood, feeling better for the thought and much more like herself. She was seldom flustered and almost never blushed and the heartbeat that had raced in her breast was an unheard-of occurrence. Perhaps it was the fight that had made her unsettled and uncertain, for she could not remember a time when she had ever heard a voice raised in such fury or men hitting out at each other. Certainly she had never seen a man in a state of such undress.

Ridiculously she hoped the stranger would have had

the sense to adjust his cravat and his jacket before he entered the main salons.

No! Her rational mind rejected such a thought. Let him be thrown out into the street and away from the city. She wondered what had happened to arouse such strong emotion in the first place. Cards, probably, and drink! She had smelt it on their clothes and her cousin's behaviour of late had been increasingly erratic, his sense of honour tarnished with a wilder anger ever since returning home to England.

Poor Lillian!

She would not think about it again. Those silly young girls had no notion of what they spoke of and she was more than happy with her life.

Lucas Clairmont draped his legs across the stool and looked into the fire burning in the grate of Nathaniel Lindsay's town house in Mayfair.

'My face will feel better come the morrow,' Lucas said, raising his glass to swallow the chilled water, the bottle nestling in an ice-bucket beside him.

'Davenport has always had a hot temper, so I'd watch your back on dark nights as you wend your way home. Especially if you are on a winning streak at the tables.'

Luc laughed. Loudly. 'I'd like to see him try it.'

'He is no lightweight, Luc. His family name affords him a position here that is…secure.'

'I'll deal with it, Nat,' he countered, glad when his friend nodded.

'His cousin, Miss Lillian Davenport, on the other hand is formidably scrupulous.'

'She's the woman I saw in the white dress?' He had already asked Nat her name as they had walked to the waiting coach and now seemed the time to find out more, her pale blue eyes and blonde hair reminding him of the lily flowers that grew in profusion near the riverbeds in Richmond, Virginia.

'Is she married?'

'No. She is famous not only for her innate good manners but also for her ability to say no to marriage proposals and, believe me, there have been many.'

Luc gingerly touched his bottom lip, which was still hurting.

'Society here is under the impression that you are a reprobate and a wild cannon, Luc. Many more tussles like tonight and you may find yourself on the outskirts of even the card games.'

Lucas shook his head. 'I barely touched him and he only got in a punch because I wasn't expecting it. Where does Lillian Davenport live, by the way?'

'We're back to her again. My God, she is as dangerous to you as her cousin and many times over more clever. A woman who all men would like to possess and who in the end wants none of them.'

Cassandra bustled into the drawing room, a steaming hot chocolate in hand.

'Take no notice of my husband, Lucas. He speaks from his own poor experience.'

'You were lining up, Nat, at one time?'

'A good seven years back now. Her first coming out it was, and long before I ever set eyes upon my Cassie.'

'And she refused you?'

'Unconditionally. She waited until I had sent her the one and only love letter I have ever written and then gave it back.'

'Better than keeping it, I should imagine.'

He nodded. 'And those famous manners relegate anything personal to the "never to be discussed again" box, which one must find encouraging.'

'So she's not a gossip?'

'Oh, far from it,' Cassie took up the conversation. 'She is the very end word in innate good breeding and perfect bearing. Every young girl who is presented at Court is reminded of her comportment and conduct and encouraged to emulate it.'

'She sounds formidable.'

Cassandra giggled and Nathaniel interrupted his wife as she went to say more. 'Lord, Cassie, enough.' He caught her arm and pulled her down on to his knee. 'Luc is only here in London until the end of December and we have much to reminisce about.'

'I'll drink to that, Nat.' Raising his glass, Luc swallowed the lot, already planning his second foray into discovering the exact character of Daniel Davenport.

Lillian pulled up the sheets on her bed and lay down with a sigh. She had left her curtains slightly open and the moon shone brightly in the space between. A full moon tonight, and the beams covered her room in silver.

She felt…excited, and could not explain the feeling even to herself, the sleep she would have liked so far, far away. Her hand slid across her stomach beneath the gossamer-thin silk nightdress.

John Wilcox-Rice had been most attentive tonight, but it was another face she sought. A darker, more dangerous countenance with laughing golden eyes and a voice from another land. Her fingers traced across her skin soft and gentle, like the path of a feather.

Bringing her hands together when she realised where they lingered, she closed her eyes and summoned sleep. But the urgency was not dimmed, rather it flared in the silver moon and in the pull of something she had no control over. A single tear ran down her temple and into her hair. Wet. Real. She was twenty-five and waiting for…what?

The stranger had tipped his head to her, night-black hair caught long in the sort of leather strap that a man from past centuries would have worn. Careless of fashion!

His hands had been forceful and brown, work imbued into the very form of them. What must it be like to have a hand like that touch her body? Not soft, not smooth. Fingers that had worked the earth hard or loved a woman well!

She smiled at such a thought, but could not quite dismiss it.

'Please…' she whispered into the night, but the entreaty itself made her pause.

'Let me find someone to love, someone to care for, someone to love me back.' Not for her money or for her clothes or for the colour of her hair, which men always admired. Not those things, she thought.

'For me. For just me.' Words diffusing into the silence of the night as the winds of winter buffeted the house and the almost full moon disappeared behind thick rain-filled clouds.

Chapter Two

Her father was at breakfast the next morning, an occurrence that was becoming more and more rare these days with the time he spent at his clubs and his new interest in horseflesh pulling him away from London for longer and longer time-spans.

'Good morning, Lillian,' he said with a lilt in his voice and her puzzlement grew. 'I have it on good authority that you had a splendid time at the Lenningtons' last night?'

A splendid time? She could not for the life of her quite fathom his meaning.

'Lord Wilcox-Rice called to see me yesterday afternoon to ask if he might court you with an eye to a betrothal later in the month and I had heard from Patrick that you spent much of the night at his side.'

Lillian grimaced at her youngest cousin's penchant for telling a tale. 'I was there as a friend.'

The words were wrung out in anger and her father's brows lifted in astonishment.

'Wilcox-Rice has not said anything to you yet? Perhaps the boy is shy or perhaps you did not encourage him as it may have been prudent to.'

'I do not wish for his advances. I could not even imagine…'

'All the best marriages begin with just that. A friendship that develops into love and lasts a lifetime.'

The unspoken words hung between them.

Like your marriage did not. Mama. A quick dalliance with an unsuitable man and then her death. Repenting it all, and an absolution never given.

'Lord Wilcox-Rice wishes for you to become better acquainted. He wants you to spend some time with him at his estate in Kent. Chaperoned, of course, but well away from London and it may give you the chance to—'

'No, Papa.'

Her father was still. The knife he held in his hand was carefully set down on his plate, the jam upon it as yet to be spread. 'I think, Lillian, we have come to an impasse, you and I. You are a girl with a strong mind, but your years are mounting and the chances you may have for a family and a home of your own are diminishing with each passing birthday.'

Lillian hated this argument. Twenty-five had pounced upon her with all the weight of expectations and conjecture; an iniquitous year when women were no longer young and could not fall back upon the easy excuse of choice.

'John Wilcox-Rice is from a good family with all the advantages of upbringing that you yourself have had. He would not wish to change you, and he would make an admirable father, something that you must be now at least thinking about.'

'But I don't have any feelings for him. Not ones that would naturally lead to marriage.'

With a quick flick of his fingers her father dismissed the servants gathered behind them. Left alone, Lillian could hear the ticking of the grandfather clock in the corner of the room, time marked by mounting seconds of silence.

Finally her father began. 'I am nearing fifty, Lillian, and my health is not as it once was. I need to know that you are settled before I am too much older. I need grand-children and the chance of an heir for Fairley Manor.'

'You speak as if I am over thirty, Father, and I can see little wrong with the state of your health.' She did not care for the harshness she heard in her voice.

'Then if you cannot understand the gist of my words, I worry about you even more.'

His tone had risen, no longer the measured evenness of logic and sense, and Lillian walked across to the window to look out over Hyde Park where a few people rode their horses on the pathways. Everything was just as it should be, whereas in here….

'I will give you till Christmas.'

'I beg your pardon?' She turned to face him.

'I will give you until Christmas to find a man of your choice to marry, and if you have no other candidate by then you must promise me to consider Wilcox-Rice and without prejudice.'

His face was blotched with redness, the weight he had put on since last year somehow more worrying than before. Was he ailing? He had seen the physician last week. Perhaps he had learnt something was not right?

Regret and remorse surged simultaneously, but she did not question him. He was a man who held his secrets and seldom divulged his thoughts. Like her, she supposed, and that made her sad.

She was cornered, by parental authority and by the part in her heart that wanted to make her ageing father happy, no matter what.

'It is not so very easy to find a man who is everything that I want.'

'Then find one who is enough, Lillian.' His retort came quickly. 'With children great happiness can follow and Wilcox-Rice is a good fellow. At least give me the benefit of the wisdom old age brings.'

'Very well, then. I will promise to consider your advice.' When she held out her hand to his, she liked the way he did not break the contact, but kept her close.

Half an hour later she was in the morning room to one side of the town house having a cup of tea with Anne Weatherby, an old friend, and trying to feign interest in the topic of her children and family, a subject that usually took up nearly all the hours of her visit. Today, however, she had other issues to discuss.

'There was a contretemps last night at Lenningtons'. Did you hear of it?'

Lillian's attention was immediately caught.

'It seems that your cousin Daniel and a stranger from America were in a scuffle of sorts. I saw him as he walked from the salon afterwards. He barely looked English, the savage ways of the backwaters imprinted on his clothes and hands and face. So dangerous and uncivilised.' She began to smile. 'And yet wildly good-looking.'

'I saw nothing.'

'Rumour has it that you did.'

'Well, perhaps I saw the very end of it all as I came from the retiring room. It was but a trifle.' She tried to look bored with the whole subject in the hope that Anne might change the topic, but was to have no such luck.

'It is said that he has a reputation in America that is hardly savoury. A Virginian, I am told, whose wife died in a way that was…suspicious at the very least.'

'Suspicious?'

'Alice, the Countess of Horsham, would say no more on the matter, but her tone of voice indicated that the fellow might have had a hand in her demise.' She shook her head before continuing. 'Although the gossip is all about town, the young girls seem much enamoured by his looks and are setting their caps at him in the hopes of even a smile. He has a dimple on his right cheek, some-thing I always found attractive in a man.' She placed her hands across her mouth and smiled through them. 'Lord, but I am running on, and at thirty I should have a lot more sense than to be swayed by a handsome face.'

Lillian poured another cup of tea for herself, while Anne had barely sipped at hers. She hoped that her friend did not see the way the liquid slopped across the side of the cup of its own accord and dribbled on to the white-lace linen cloth beneath it. How easy it was to be tipped from this place to that one. His wife. Dead!

Her imaginings in a bed bathed in moonlight took on a less savoury feel and she pushed down disappointment.

No man had ever swept her off her feet in all the seven years she had been out and to imagine that this one had even the propensity to do so suddenly seemed silly. Of course a man who looked like this American would not be a fit companion for her with his raw and rough manner and his dangerous eyes. The promise she had made her father less than an hour ago surfaced and she shook away the ridiculous yearnings.

Betrothed by Christmas! Ah well, she thought as she guided the conversation to a more general one, if worst came to the worst, John Wilcox-Rice was at least biddable and she *was* past twenty-five.

She met John at a party that evening in Belgrave Square and she knew that she was in trouble as soon as she saw his face. He looked excited and nervous at the same time, his smile both protective and concerned. When he took her fingers in his own she was glad for her gloves and glad too for the ornamental shrubbery placed beside the orchestra. It gave her a chance to escape the prying eyes of others while she tried to explain it all to him.

When the cornet, violin and cello proved too much to speak over she pulled him out on to the balcony a little further away from the room, where the light was dimmer, the shadow of the shrubs throwing a kinder glow on both their faces.

'You had my message from your father, then, about my interest—' he began, but she allowed him no further discourse.

'I certainly did and I thank you for the compliment, but I do not think we could possibly—'

'Your father thinks differently,' he returned, and a sneaking suspicion started to well in Lillian's breast.

'You have seen my father today?' she began, stopping as he nodded.

'Indeed I have and he was at pains to tell me you had agreed to at least consider my proposal.'

'But I do not hold the sort of feelings for you that you would want, and there would be no guarantee that I ever could.'

'I know.' He took her hand again, this time peeling back the fine silk of her right glove, and pressing his lips to her wrist. Without meaning to she dragged her hand away, wiping it on the generous fabric of her skirt and thinking that this meeting place might not have been the wisest one after all.

'I just want you to at least try. I want the chance to make you happy and I think that we would rub along together rather nicely.'

'Well,' she returned briskly, 'I certainly value your friendship and I would indeed be very loath to lose it, but as for the rest....'

He bowed before her. 'I understand and I am ready to give you more time to ponder over it, Lillian, for as like-minded people of a similar birth I am convinced such a union would benefit us both.'

She nodded and watched as he clicked his heels together and took his leave, a tall, thin man who was passably good looking and infinitely suitable. A husband she could indeed grow old with in a fairly satisfying relationship.

Sighing, she made her way to the edge of the balcony, the same moon as the night before mocking her in her movements, remembering.

'Stop it!' she admonished herself out loud.

'Stop what?' Another voice answered and the American walked out from the shrubs behind her, the red tip of a cheroot the only thing standing out from the black of his silhouette.

'How long have you been there?'

'Long enough.'

'A gentleman would have walked away.'

He pointedly looked across the balustrade. 'The fifteen-foot drop is somewhat of a deterrent.'

'Or stayed quiet until I had left.' The beat of her heart

was worrying, erratic, hard. 'Why, most Englishmen would be mortified to find themselves in this situation…' She didn't finish, owing to a loud laugh that rang rich in the night air.

'Mortified?' he repeated. 'It has been a long while since I last felt that.' His accent was measured tonight and at times barely heard, a different voice from the one he had affected at the Lenningtons' with its broad Virginian drawl. She was glad she could not catch his eyes, still shaded by the greenery, though in the position she stood she knew her own to be well on show.

Perhaps he had orchestrated it so? The gold band on the ring finger of his left hand jolted her. His marriage finger! She tried not to let him see where she looked.

'We have not even been introduced, sir. None of this can be in any way proper. You must repair inside this instant.'

Still he did not move, the dimple that Anne Weatherby had spoken of dancing in his cheek.

'I am Lucas Clairmont from Richmond in Virginia,' he said finally. 'And you are Miss Davenport, a woman of manners and good taste, though I wonder at the wisdom of Wilcox-Rice as a groom?'

'He is not that. You just heard me tell him so.'

'He and your father seem to believe otherwise.' Now he walked straight into the light and the golden eyes that had haunted her dreams made her pause. She swallowed heavily and held her hands hard against her thighs to stop them from shaking, though when he picked a slender stem from a pyracanthus bush behind him and handed it to her she leant forwards to take it.

'Thank you.' She could think of nothing else at all to say. The thorn on the stem pricked the base of her thumb.

'I am glad I have this chance to apologise for frightening you yesterday at the Lenningtons'.'

'Apology accepted.' For the first time some of her tension dissipated with the simple reasoning that a criminal mind would not run to seeking any sort of amnesty. 'I realise that my cousin can be rather trying at times.'

His teeth were white against the brown of his face and Lillian was jolted back to reality as his eyes darkened and she saw for a moment a man she barely recognised.

A dangerous man. A man who would not be moulded or conditioned by the society in which he found himself.

So unlike her. She stepped back, afraid now of a thing that she had no name for, and wondered what her cousin had done to cause such enmity.

'Have no fear, Miss Davenport. I would not kill him because he's not worth being hanged at Newgate for.'

Kill him? My God. To even think that he might consider it and then qualify any lack of action with a personal consequence.

I would if I could get away with it.

John Wilcox-Rice's gentle mediocrity began to look far more appealing until Luc Clairmont reached out for her hand and took it in his own. The shock of contact left her mute, but against her will she was drawn to him.

Against her will? She could not even say that!

His finger traced the lines on her palm and then the veins that showed through in the pale skin of her wrist.

'An old Indian woman read my hand once in Richmond. She told me that life was like a river and that we are taken by the currents to a place we are meant to be.'

His amber eyes ran across hers, the humour once again back. 'Is this that place, Miss Davenport?'

Time seemed to stop, frozen into moonlight and want and warmth. When she snatched her hand away and almost ran inside, she could have sworn it was laughter she heard, following her from a balcony drenched in silver.

She stopped walking quite so briskly once she was back amongst others, finding a certain safety in numbers that she had never felt the need of before. Would he come again and speak to her? Would he create a fuss? The very thought had her hauling her fan from her reticule, to waft it to and fro, the breeze engendered calming her a little. She stuffed the sprig of orange berries into her velvet bag, glad to have them out of her fingers where someone might comment upon them.

'Your colour is rather high, Lillian,' her aunt Jean said as she joined her. 'I do hope you are not sickening for something so close to the Yuletide season. Why, Mrs Haugh was saying to me just the other day how her daughter has contracted a bronchial complaint that just cannot be shaken and…'

But Lillian was listening no more, for Lucas Clairmont had just walked in from the balcony, a tall broad-shouldered man who made the other gentlemen here look…mealy, precious and dandified. No, she must not think like that! Concentrating instead on the mark around his bottom lip that suggested another fight, she tried to ignore the way all the women in his path watched him beneath covert hooded glances.

He was leaving with the Earl of St Auburn and a man she knew to be Lord Stephen Hawkhurst. Well-placed men with the same air of menace that he had. The fact interested her and she wondered just how it was they knew each other.

As they reached the door, however, Lucas Clairmont looked straight into her eyes, tipping his head as she had seen him do at the Lenningtons' ball. Hating the way her heartbeat flared, Lillian spread her fan wide and hid her face from his, a breathless wonder overcoming caution as a game, of which she had no notion of the rules, was begun.

Once home herself she placed the crumpled orange pyracanthus in a single bloom vase and stood it on the small table by her bed. Both the colour and the shape clashed with everything else in her bedroom. As out of place in her life as Lucas Clairmont was, a vibrant interloper who conformed to neither position nor venue. Her finger reached out to carefully touch the hard nubs of thorn that marched down its stem. Forbidding. Protective. Unexpected in the riot of colour above it!

She wished she had left it on the balcony, discarded

and cast aside, as she should be doing with the thoughts of the man who had picked it. But she had not and here it was with pride of place in a room that looked as if it held its breath with nervousness. Her eyes ran over the sheer lawn drapes about her bed, the petit-point bedcover upon it in limed cream and the lamp next to her, its chalky base topped by a faded and expensive seventeenth-century tapestry. The décor in her room was nothing like the fashion of the day with its emphasis on stripes and paisleys and the busy tones of purple and red. But she enjoyed the difference.

All had been carefully chosen and were eminently suitable, like the clothes she wore and the friends she fostered. Her life. Not haphazard or risky, neither arbitrary nor disorganised.

Once it had been, once when her mother had come home to tell them that she was leaving that very afternoon *'to find excitement and adventure in the arms of a man who was thrilling'*. The very words used still managed to make her feel slightly sick, as she remembered a young girl who had idolised her mother. She was not *thrilling* and so she had been left behind, an only child whose recourse to making her father happy was to be exactly the daughter he wanted. She had excelled in her lessons and in her deportment, and later still when she came out at eighteen she had been daubed an 'original', her sense of style and quiet stillness copied by all the younger ladies at Court.

Usually she liked that. Usually she felt a certain pride

in the way she handled everything with such easy acumen. But today with the berries waving their overblown and unrestrained shapes in her room, a sense of disquiet also lingered.

Poor Lillian.

John Wilcox-Rice and his eminently sensible proposal.

Her father's advancing age.

The pieces of her life were not quite adding up to a cohesive whole any longer, and she could pin the feeling directly to Lucas Clairmont with his easy smile and his dangerous predatory eyes.

Standing by the window, she saw an outline of herself reflected in the glass. As pale as the colours in her room, perhaps, and fading. Was she her mother's daughter right down to the fact of finding her own 'thrilling and unsuitable man'? She laid her palm against the glass and, on removing it, wrote her mother's initials in the misted print

Rebecca Davenport had returned in the autumn, a thinner and sadder version of the woman who had left them, and although her father had taken her back into his house he had never taken her back into his heart. No one had known of her infidelity. The extended holiday to the Davenports' northern estate of Fairley Manor was never explained and, although people had their suspicions, the steely correctness of Ernest Davenport had meant that they were never even whispered.

Perhaps that had made things even harder, Lillian thought. The constant charade and pretence as her mother lay dying with an ague of the soul and she, a child who went between her parents with the necessary messages, seeing any respect that they had once had for each other wither with the onset of winter.

Even the funeral had been a sham, her mother's body laid in the crypt of the Davenports with all the ceremony expected, and then left unvisited.

No, the path Rebecca had taken had alienated her from everybody and should her daughter be so foolish as to follow in those footsteps she could well see the consequences of 'thrilling'.

John Wilcox-Rice was a man who would never break her heart. A constant man of sound morals and even sounder political persuasions. One hand threaded through her hair and she smiled unwillingly at the excitement that coursed through her. Everything seemed different. More tumultuous. Brighter. She walked across to the bed and ran a finger across the smooth orange berries, liking the fact that Lucas Clairmont had touched them just as she was now.

Silly thoughts. Girlish thoughts.

She was twenty-five, for goodness' sake, and a woman who had always looked askance at those highly strung débutantes whose emotions seemed to rule them. The invitation to the Cholmondeley ball on the sill caught her attention and she lifted it up. Would the American be attending this tomorrow? Perhaps he might ask her to dance? Perhaps he might lift up her hand to his again?

She shook her head and turned away as a maid came to help her get ready for bed.

Chapter Three

Luc spent the morning with a lawyer from the City signing documents and hating every single signature he marked the many pages with.

The estate of Woodruff Abbey in Bedfordshire was a place he neither wanted nor deserved and his wife's cries as she lay dying in Charlottesville, Virginia, were louder here than they had been in all the months since he had killed her.

He did not wish for the house or the chattels. He wanted to walk away and let the memories lie because recollection had the propensity to rekindle all that was gone.

Shaking away introspection, he made himself smile, a last armour against the ghosts that dragged him down.

'Will you be going up to look the old place over, Sir?'

'Perhaps.' Non-committal. Evasive.

'It is just if you wish me to accompany you, I would need to make plans.'

'No. That will not be necessary.' If he went, he would go alone.

'The servants, of course, still take retainers paid for by the rental of the farming land, though in truth the place has been let go badly.'

'I see.' He wanted just to leave. Just to take the papers and leave.

'Your wife's sister's daughters are installed in the house. Their mother died late last year and I wrote to you—'

Luc looked up. 'I did not have any such missive.'

The lawyer rifled through a sheath of sheets and, producing a paper, handed it across to him. 'Is this not your handwriting, sir?' A frown covered his brow.

With his signature staring up at him, Luc could do nothing else but nod.

'How old are these children?'

'Eight and ten, sir, and both girls.'

'Where is their father?'

'He left England a good while back and never returned. He was a violent man and, if I were to guess, I would say he lies in a pauper's grave somewhere, unmarked and uncared for. Charity and Hope are, however, the sort of girls their names suggest, and as soon as they gain their majority they will have no more claim to any favours from the Woodruff Abbey funds.'

Luc placed the paper down on the table before him. So poor-spirited, he thought, to do your duty up to a certain point and then decline further association. He had seen it time and time again in his own father, the action of being seen to have done one's duty more important than any benefit to those actively involved.

Unexpectedly he thought of Lillian Davenport. Would she be the same? he wondered, and hoped not. Last night when he had run his fingers across the pale skin on her wrist he had felt her heartbeat accelerate markedly and seen the flush that covered her cheeks before she had turned and run from him.

Not all the ice queen then, her high moral standards twisted against his baser want. Because he *had* wanted her, wanted to bring his hands along the contours of her face and her breasts and her hips hidden beneath her fancy clothing and distance.

Lord, was he stupid?

He should not have made his presence known. Should not have sparred with her or held her fingers and read her palm, for Lillian Davenport was the self-styled keeper of worthiness and he needed to stay away from her.

Yet she pierced a place in him that he had long thought of as dead, the parts of himself that he used to like, the parts that the past weeks of sobriety had begun to thaw against the bone-cold guilt that had torn at his soul.

The law books lined up against the far wall dusty in today's thin sun called him back. Horatio Thackeray was now detailing the process of the transfer of title.

Woodruff Abbey was his! He turned the gold ring on his wedding finger and pressed down hard.

* * *

Lillian enjoyed the afternoon taking tea in Regent Street with Anne Weatherby and her husband Allen. His brother Alistair had joined them, too, a tall and pleasant man.

'I have lived in Edinburgh for a good few years now,' he explained when she asked him why she had not met him before. 'I have land there and prefer the quieter pace of life.' Catching sight of a shopkeeper trying to prop up a Christmas tree in his window, he laughed. 'Queen Victoria has certainly made the season fashionable. Do you decorate a tree, Miss Davenport?'

'Oh, more than one, Mr Weatherby. I often have three or four in the town house.'

'And I am certain that you would do so with great aplomb if my sister-in-law's comments on your sense of style are to be taken into consideration.' He smiled and moved closer. 'If I could even be so bold as to ask for permission to accompany Anne to see these Yuletide trees next time she visits, I would be most grateful.'

The man was flirting with her, Lillian suddenly thought, and averted her eyes. Catching the glance of Anne at her side, she realised immediately that her friend was in on the plot.

Another man thrust beneath her nose. Another suitor who wanted a better acquaintance. All of a sudden she wished that it could have been just this easy. An instant attraction to a man who was suitable. The very thought made her tired. Perhaps she was never destined to be a wife or a mother.

'You're very quiet, Lillian?' Anne took her hand as they walked towards the waiting coach.

'I have a lot to think about.'

'I hope that Alistair is one of those thoughts?' she whispered back wickedly, laughing as Lillian made absolutely no answer. 'Would he not do just as well as Wilcox-Rice? His holdings are substantial and Scotland is a beautiful place.'

The tree in the window was suddenly hoisted into position with the sound of cheering, a small reminder of her father's ultimatum of choosing a groom before Christmas. Lillian placed a tight smile across her face.

'I am not so desperate as to throw myself on a stranger, Anne, no matter how nice he is and I would prefer it if you would not meddle.'

The joy had quite gone out of the afternoon and she hated the answering annoyance in her oldest friend's eyes. But today she could not help it. She had not been sleeping well, dreams of Virginia and the dark-haired American haunting her slumber, the remembered feel of his thumb tracing the beat on her wrist and the last sight of him tipping his head as he had left the room in the company of his friends.

To compare Lucas Clairmont to these other men was like equating the light made by tiny fireflies to that of the full-blown sun, a man whom she had never met the measure of before in making her aware that she was a woman. Breathing out heavily, she held on to her composure and answered a question Alistair asked her with all the eagerness that she could muster.

Chapter Four

$\sim\!\!\!\sim\!\!\!\sim\!\!\!\sim$

The gown Lillian wore to the Cholmondeley ball was one of her favourites, a white satin dress with wide petticoats looped with tulle flowers. The train was of glacé and moiré silk, the festoons on the edge plain but beautiful. Her hair was entwined with a single strand of diamonds and these were mirrored in the quiet beading on her bodice. She seldom wore much ornamentation, preferring an understated elegance, and virtually always favoured white.

The ball was in full swing when she arrived with her father and aunt after ten; the suites of rooms on the first floor of the town house were opened up to each other and the floor in the long drawing room was polished until it shone. At the top of the chamber sat a substantial orchestra, and within it a group of guests that would have numbered well over four hundred.

'James Cholmondeley is harking for the renommée

of a crush,' her father murmured as they made their way inside. 'Let us hope that the champagne, at least, is of good quality.'

'He must be of the persuasion that it is of benefit to be remembered in London, whether good or ill.' Her aunt Jean's voice was louder than Lillian would have liked it. 'And I do hope that your dress is not hopelessly wrecked in such a crowd, my dear, and that the floor does not mark your satin slippers.' She looked up as she spoke. 'At least they have replaced the candles in the chandeliers with globe lamps so we are not to be burned.'

Lillian was not listening to her aunt's seemingly endless list of complaints. To her the chamber looked beautiful, with its long pale-yellow banners and fresh flowers. The late-blooming roses were particularly lovely, she thought, as she scanned the room.

Was Lucas Clairmont here already? He was taller than a great deal of the other gentlemen present so he might not be too hard to find.

John Wilcox-Rice's arm on hers made her start. 'I have been waiting for you to come, Lillian. I thought indeed that you might have been at the MacLay ball in Mayfair.'

'No, we went to the Manners's place in Belgrave Square.'

'I had toyed with the idea of going there myself, but Andrew MacLay is a special friend of mine and I had promised him my patronage.' A burst of music from the orchestra caught his attention as the instruments were tuned. 'The quadrille should be beginning soon. May I have the pleasure of escorting you through it?'

Her heart sank at his request, but manners forced her to smile. 'Of course,' she said, marking her dance card with his name.

The lead-off dance might give her the chance to look more closely at the patrons of this ball, as the pace of the thing was seldom faster than a walk and Lucas Clairmont as an untitled stranger would not be able to take his place at the top of the ballroom without offending everyone.

Her heart began to beat faster. Would he know of those rules? Would he be aware of such social ostracism should he try to invade a higher set? Lord, the things that had until tonight never worried her began to eat at her composure.

Still as yet she had not seen him, though she supposed a card room to be set up somewhere. She unfurled her fan, enjoying the cool air around her face and hoped that he would not surprise her with his presence.

The quadrille was called almost immediately and Lillian walked to the top of the room, using up some of the small talk that was the first necessity for dancing it as she went.

Holding her skirt out a little, she began the *chasser*, the sedate tempo of the steps allowing conversation.

'Are you in London for the whole of the Yule season?' Wilcox-Rice asked her, and she shook her head.

'No, we will repair to Fairley in the first week of January and stay down till February. Papa is keen to see how his new horses race and has employed the services of a well-thought-of jockey in his quest to be included in next year's Derby Day at Epsom. And you?' Feeling it only polite, she asked him the same question back.

'Your father asked me down after Twelfth Night. Did he not tell you?'

Lillian shook her head.

'If you would rather I declined, you just need to say the word.'

She was saved answering by the complicated steps of the dance spiriting her away from him. The elderly gentleman she now faced smiled, but remained silent; taking her lead from him she was glad for the respite.

Luc watched Lillian Davenport from his place behind a colonnade at the foot of the room. He had seen her enter, seen the rush of men surround her asking for a dance and Wilcox-Rice placing his hand across hers to draw her away from them. Her father was there, too; Nat had pointed him out and an older woman whom he presumed was a family member. She seemed to be grumbling about something above her and Luc supposed it must be the lighting. Lillian looked as she always did, unapproachable and elegant. He noticed how the women around her covertly looked over her dress, a shining assortment of shades of white material cascading across a lacy petticoat.

She had worn white every single time he had seen her and the colour mirrored the paleness of her skin and hair.

He smiled at his own ruminations. Lord, when had he ever noticed what a woman had worn before? The mirth died a little as he thought about the ramifications of such awareness. With determination he turned away, the quadrille and its ridiculous rules taking up the whole of the upper ballroom. British aristocracy took itself so seriously; in Virginia such unwritten social codes would be laughed about and ignored. Here, however, he did not wish for the bother of making his point. In less than two months he would be on a ship sailing back to America where the nonsensical and exclusive dances of the upper classes in London would be only a memory.

The chatter of voices around him made him turn and Nathaniel introduced two very pretty sisters to him, the elder laying her hand across his arm and showing him a card that she had, the dances named on one side and a few blank spaces that were not filled in with pencil upon the other.

'I have a polka free still, sir. If you should like to ask me…'

Nat laughed beside him. 'I have been fending off interested ladies since you arrived, Luc. Do me at least the courtesy of filling your night so that I have no further need of mediation and diplomacy.'

Cornered, Luc assented though it had been a long time since he had learned the steps to the thing. A complicated dance, he remembered, though not as fast as the galop. He wished he had taken better heed of his teacher's instructions when he had been a lad, and

wished also that it might have been Lillian Davenport
that he partnered.

The girl's younger sister thrust her own card at him
and he was glad when they finally turned to leave.

Lord, time was beginning to run short and he did not
want to be in England any longer than he had to be.

A flash of Lillian caught his eye as she finished with
the quadrille and bowed to her partner. Finally it looked
as though Wilcox-Rice might depart of his own accord
and that he could get at least a little conversation with
the most beautiful woman in the room.

But when another man claimed her for the waltz he
admitted defeat and moved into the next salon to see
what could be had in the way of supper.

The dancing programme was almost halfway
through and Lillian was quite exhausted. She had deliberately pencilled in two waltzes with made-up initials
just in case Luc Clairmont should show, but by midnight
was giving up the hope of seeing him here.

Sir Richard Graham, a man who had pursued her
several years earlier and one she had never warmed to,
had asked her for the third galop and she had just taken
her place in the circle when she felt a strange tingle
along the back of her neck.

He was here, she was sure of it, the shock of connection as vivid as it had been on first seeing him outside
the retiring room at the Lenningtons'.

Gritting her teeth, she took four steps forwards as her

partner took her left hand in his, and when she moved
back again she casually looked across her shoulder.

He was three or four couples behind them, partner-
ing a pretty girl whom she knew to be the younger one
of the Parker sisters and he looked for all the world as
if he might actually be enjoying the dance. Certainly the
Parker girl was, her colour high and her eyes flashing,
the dimples in her cheeks easily on show.

Perhaps he had been here all night and made no effort
to single her out. Perhaps this sharp knowledge she felt
when he was near her was not reciprocated. Stepping
forwards, she gained in ground on the couple in front
of her and Graham's hand closed upon her own, slowing
her down. Concentrate, she admonished herself. Concentrate and pretend that Lucas Clairmont is not there,
that you do not care for him, this reckless colonial who
can only do your reputation harm.

For the next few figures in the dance she felt her confidence return, then drain away altogether as he winked
at her when she caught his eyes across the small space
between them. She turned away quickly, not deigning
any reply, and listened to some inconsequential thing her
partner was relaying to her, trying to give the impression of the free-and-fancy woman she did not feel at all.
When the dance ended she curtsied and allowed Graham
to take her hand and lead her back to the shelter of her
aunt, a courtesy she rarely took part in.

'You look flushed, my dear,' Jean said as she finished
off a sizeable glass of lemonade, followed by a straw-

berry bonbon. The first strains of a waltz filled the air and Lillian looked at her card. The initials she had written there stared back at her.

'Your partner for this next dance is rather tardy.' Aunt Jean looked around expectantly. 'Ahh, here he is now.'

Lillian's head whipped upwards as Luc Clairmont strode into view beside them, and again she was mesmerised by his reckless golden eyes.

'Miss Davenport,' he said before turning to her companion. 'Ma'am.'

Her aunt's mouth had dropped open, the red of the strawberry bonbon strangely marking her tongue.

'Aunt Jean, let me introduce you to Mr Lucas Clairmont, from America. Mr Clairmont this is my aunt, Lady Taylor-Reid.'

Again Luc bowed his head. 'Pleased to meet you, ma'am.'

Her aunt flushed strangely. 'How long have you been in England, Mr Clairmont?'

'Only a few weeks'

'Do you like it?'

'Indeed I do.' He looked straight at her, the dimple in his cheek deeper than she had seen it, the gold of his eyes glinting in mirth.

The music had now begun in earnest, the dance getting underway and, excusing herself, she allowed Lucas to guide her through the throngs of people.

On the floor his hand laced around her waist and she felt the warmth of it like a burn. In England it was proper for couples to stand a good foot apart, but the American way seemed different as he brought her close, his free hand taking her fingers and clasping them tight.

'I had thought I would have no chance for a waltz with you, Lillian. How is it that your card is empty on the best dance of them all?'

She ignored his familiar use of her name, reasoning that as no one else had heard him use it, it could do no harm.

'It was a mix-up,' she replied as they swirled effortlessly around the room. He was a good dancer! No wonder the Parker sister had looked so thrilled.

'Are there other mix-ups on your card?'

She laughed, surprised by his candour. 'Actually, I have the last waltz free...'

'Pencil me in,' he replied, sweeping her around the top corner of the room, her petticoat swirling to one side with the movement of it, an elation building that she had never before felt in dancing.

Safe. Strong. The outline of his muscles could be seen against the black of his jacket and felt in the hard power of his thighs. A man who had not grown up in the salons of courtly life but in a tougher place of work and need. Even his clothes mirrored a disregard for the height of fashion, his jacket not the best of cuts and his shoes a dull matt black. Just a 'little dressed,' she thought, his apparel of a make that held no pretension to arrogance or ornament. She saw that he had tied his neckcloth simply and that his gloves were removed.

She wished she had done the same and then she

might feel the touch of his skin against her own, but the thought withered with the onslaught of his next words.

'I am bound for Virginia before too much longer. I have passage on a ship in late December and, if the seas are kind, I may see Hampton by the middle of February.'

'Hampton is your home?' She tried to keep the question light and her disappointment hidden.

'No. My place is up on the James River, near Richmond.'

'And your family?'

When he did not answer and the light in his eyes dimmed with her words, she tried another tack. 'I had a friend once who left London for a home in Philadelphia. Is that somewhere near?'

'Somewhere…' he answered, whirling her around one last time before the music stopped. Bowing to her as their hands dropped away from each other, he asked, 'May I escort you back to your aunt? Your father does not look too happy with my dancing style.'

Lillian smiled and did not look over at her father for fear that he might beckon her back. 'No. I have not supped yet and find myself hungry.'

The break in the music allowed him the luxury of choice. If he wanted to slip away he could, and if he wanted to accompany her to the supper room he had only to take her arm. She was pleased when he did that, allowing herself to be manoeuvred towards the refreshment room.

Once there she was at a loss as to what to say next,

his admission of travelling home so soon having taken the wind from her sails. She saw the Parker girls and their friends behind him some little distance away and noticed that they watched her intently.

When he handed her a plate she thanked him, though he did not take one, helping himself to a generous drink of lemonade instead.

'Are you in London over Christmas?' His question was one she had been asked all the night, a conversation topic of little real value and, when compared to the communion they had enjoyed the last time of meeting, disappointing.

She nodded. 'We usually repair to Fairley Manor, our country seat in Hertfordshire, in the first week of January.' When he smiled all of the magic returned in a flood.

'Nathaniel Lindsay is to give a house party at his country estate in Kent on the weekend of November the twentieth. Will you be there?'

'The Earl of St Auburn? I do not know if I have an invite…'

'I could send you one.'

Shock mixed with delight and ran straight through into the chambers of her heart.

'It is not proper.'

'But you will come anyway?'

He did not move closer or raise his voice, he did not reach out for her hand or brush his arm against her own as he so easily could here at this crowded refreshment table, and because of it, the invite was even the more clandestine. Real. A measure taken to transport her from this place to another one.

An interruption by the Countess of Horsham meant that she could not answer him, and when he excused himself from their company she let him go, fixing her glance upon the tasteless biscuit on her plate.

Alice watched him, however, and the smile on her lips was unwelcome. 'I had heard you witnessed the fellow in a contretemps the other evening? Do you know him, Lillian, know anything of his family and his living?'

'Just a little. He is a good friend of the Earl of St Auburn.'

'Indeed. There are other rumours that I have heard, too. It seems he may have inherited a substantial property on the death of his wife. Some say he is here to collect that inheritance and leave again, more gold for his gambling habit and the fracas with your cousin still unresolved. Less kind folks would say that he killed the woman to get the property and that his many children out of wedlock are installed in the place.'

'Are you warning me, Countess?

'Do I need to, Lillian?'

'No.' She bit down on the lemon biscuit and washed away the dryness with chilled tea, the taste combined as bitter as the realisation that she was being watched. And watched carefully.

Of course she could not go to Kent even if she had wanted to. Pretending a headache, she excused herself from the Countess's company, and went to find her aunt.

* * *

Luc saw her leave, the ball still having at least an hour left and the promised last dance turning to dust. The Countess of Horsham's husband was a man he had met at the card tables and a gossip of the first order. Lord, the tale of his own poor reputation had probably reached Lillian and he doubted that she would countenance such a lack of morals. Perhaps it was for the best. Perhaps the 'very good' had a God-given inbuilt mechanism of protection that fended off people like him, a celestial safeguard that separated the chaff from the wheat.

When the oldest Parker sister obstructed his passage on the pretext of claiming him in the next dance, he made himself smile as he escorted the girl on to the floor.

Once home Lillian checked the week's invitations scattered on the hall table. When she found none from the Earl of St Auburn, she relaxed. No problem to mull over and dither about, no temptation to answer in the affirmative and have her heart broken completely. She remembered her last sight of Lucas Clairmont flirting with the pretty Parker heiress she had seen him with earlier in the evening, the same smile he had bequeathed her wide across his face.

On gaining her room, she snatched the stupid orange pyracanthus from the vase near her bed and threw it into the fire burning brightly in the grate. A few of the berries fell off in their flight, and she picked them up, squeezing them angrily and liking the way the juice of blushed red stained her hand.

She would invite Wilcox-Rice to call on her tomorrow and make an effort to show some kindness. Such an act would please her father and allay the fears of her aunt who had regaled her all the way home on the ills of marrying improperly and the ruin that could follow.

Lillian wondered how much her father had told his only sister about the downfall of his wife and was glad, at least, that Aunt Jean had had the sense not to mention any such knowledge to her. Indeed, she needed to regain her balance, her equanimity and her tranquil demeanour and to do that she needed to stay well away from Lucas Clairmont.

Chapter Five

Woodruff Abbey, in Bedfordshire, was old, a house constructed in the days when the classical lines of architecture had been in their heyday, early seventeenth century or late sixteenth. Now it just looked tired, the colonnades in the portico chipped and rough and numerous windows boarded in places, as though the glass had been broken and was not able to be repaired. The thought puzzled him—the income of this place was well able to cover expenses towards the upkeep and day-to-day running, according to Thackeray, his lawyer. Why then had it been left to look so rundown?

At the front door he stopped and looked at the garden stretching from the house to the parkland below and the polluted business of London seemed far away. Breathing in, he smiled, and the tense anger of the past few years seemed to recede a bit, the faded elegance of the Abbey soothing in its dishevelled beauty.

The door was suddenly pulled open and a man stood there. An old man, whose hat was placed low upon his head and whose eyes held the rheumy glare of one who could in truth barely see.

'May I be of assistance, sir?' His cultured voice was surprising.

'I am Lucas Clairmont. I hope that Mr Thackeray has sent you word of my coming.'

'The lawyer? Clairmont? Lord! You are here already?'

'I am.' Luc waited. The man did not move from his place in the middle of the doorway, his knuckles clutching white at the lintel as though he might fall.

'The Mr Clairmont from America?'

'Indeed.' He bit back a smile. Was he going to be invited into his own house or not?

'Who is there, Jack? Who is at the door? Tell them that we need nothing.'

A woman appeared behind him, a woman every bit as old as he was, her shawl wrapped tightly across a thin frame, spectacles balancing on her nose.

'It is Mr Clairmont, Lizzie. Mr Clairmont, this is my wife, Mrs Poole'

Her eyes widened behind the glasses and the frown that had been there when he first saw her thickened.

'We had word, of course, but we had not thought…'

Her words petered out as she stood beside her husband, both of them now looking across at his person as if they could not quite believe he was there.

'May I come in?'

The request sent them into a whirl of activity and as the door was thrown wide open they stepped back.

The wide central portico was open to the roof, and the oversized windows let in a generous amount of light. He noticed that the floors were well scrubbed and that the banisters and woodwork had been polished until they shone. Not an unloved house, then, but one strapped by the lack of cash.

'We are Jack and Lizzie Poole, sir,' the woman said once the door was again fastened, 'and we have served this estate for nigh on a century between us.'

Luc nodded, easily believing the length of time stated.

'And where are the other servants who help you?'

'Other servants, sir?' Puzzlement showed on their brows.

'The cook and the governess, the maids and the grooms. Where are they?'

'It's only us, sir, and it has been for a very long time.'

'But there are children here?'

Both their eyes lit up. 'Indeed there are. Miss Charity and Miss Hope and good girls they are at that.'

'Who teaches them, then? Who sees to their lessons?'

'There is nobody else.'

'So I am to understand that it is just you and the two girls who live here and have done so for some months?'

'Almost twelve months, sir, since the money stopped coming and they all up and left! Not us though, we could not stand around and see the wee ones homeless.'

Luc took in a breath and he swore he would visit

Thackeray the instant he returned to town in order to get to the bottom of just where the funds had gone.

'Where are the children? Could they be brought down?'

'Down, sir?'

'From the nursery?'

'Oh, goodness gracious, they are seldom there. If it is a fine day they will be down by the lake, and if it is a wet one in their hut near the trees.'

This time he did laugh. Two little girls without the weight of the English society rules upon them promised to be interesting indeed. His own childhood had been much the same, a violent father whom he saw only intermittently and a mother who was never well. Perhaps these old people would have been an improvement!

A noise from one end of the hall had them turning and a child stood there. A thin pale child with the shortest hair he had ever seen on a girl of her age and large blue eyes.

'Charity,' Mrs Poole said as she walked forwards. 'You are back early. Come and meet Mr Clairmont, dear, for he is just come from London.'

The girl's teeth worried her bottom lip and her light glance was full of anxiety, but she allowed the woman to shuffle her forwards.

'She does not speak as such since the passing of her mother, sir, but she will certainly know you.'

Did not speak? He had had little to do with children in his life and was at a loss as to how to deal with this one. Still he tried his best. 'I would like to see your tree house one day.'

She nodded. At least she understood him without lip reading, her eyes trained upon the floor.

'Her sister, Hope, will not be in till after dark. Will you be staying, sir?'

He wondered what Hope did for all of the hours of daylight, but with the lack of concern on all the faces before him refrained from asking the question.

'I have not booked passage back to London until the morrow and I think there is much to discuss about this situation.'

Lizzie Poole looked at her husband and Charity clutched the old lady's hand tighter, Luc calculating in a second that although there was not a lot here in the way of material richness, love was apparent. For that at least he was glad.

'Jack here will see you to your room, Mr Lucas, and I will go to the kitchen to prepare some dinner. Charity love, will you give me a hand?'

When the child smiled the sun came out, her deep dimples etched into her cheeks and blue eyes dancing with laughter. A beauty, he thought suddenly, and Lillian Davenport came to mind. This girl had her sort of timeless elegance, even dressed as she was in a gown about two sizes too small and patched everywhere. He wondered what the sister would look like as he followed Jack Poole up the solid oak staircase.

Dinner consisted of two tiny cooked carcases he presumed to be wild fowl, a bowl full of boiled potatoes and a handful of greenery that looked like the watercress farmers in Virginia grew by the James.

'The land provideth and the Lord taketh away,' Mrs Poole told him sagely as they sat at a table in the kitchen, the fire in the oven behind a welcome asset to keep out the cold.

Hope was still outside, he presumed, as her place was empty. Charity sat next to him, her hands folded in her lap as she waited for grace to be said. A long and complex prayer of thanks it turned out to be too, a good five minutes having passed as Lizzie Poole gave acknowledgement for all the things that God had sent them, for their health and hearth and laughter, for the fuel which fed the fire and the earth which supported them. To Luc's mind she seemed a trifle generous in her praise, the fowl in particular looking like they had seen but three months of life and barely eaten anything in that time. Still, it was refreshing to see gratefulness in small blessings and he wondered what she might say of the overladen London tables should she ever see them.

Just as they had finished the kitchen door banged open and an older child walked in. She looked nothing like her sister, except for her thin build, her hair a wild tangle of long deep brown curls and her skin darkened by the sun.

'I am sorry to be so late, Lizzie,' she said, stopping as bright emerald eyes met his own. Another beauty, but of a different mould.

'This is Mr Lucas Clairmont, Hope. He has come from London today to see you and your sister.'

Hope's eyes went to Charity's and a communication passed between them. A silent language of perception and accord.

'Very pleased to meet you, sir.' She curtsied in a way reminiscent of another age.

'Mrs Poole tells me you spend a lot of time outdoors. What things do you do there?'

'We fish sometimes for the dinner table, and collect this cress. If we are lucky, we bag hares or wild birds and in the spring we steal the eggs from the nests that are low in the hedgerows.'

'So this bounty is your doing?' he replied, gesturing to the food on the table.

'Some of it is, sir. Winter is the most difficult time to gather, but come spring we can find all sorts of berries and mushrooms and even wild tomatoes.'

'So your sister helps you?'

'Of course.' She flashed a smile and the other nodded. Tonight Charity appeared a lot more worried than she had a few hours ago but Hope picked up quickly on her fright, settling herself on the other side of the girl and again that wordless communication that excluded everyone in the room.

'They are very close, sir. If anyone were to split them up…'

'I have not come here to do that.'

'This house is the only home they have ever known and were they to be thrown out…'

'I have not come to do that, either.'

'Their mother was perhaps a trifle wild, I realise that, but Charity and Hope have never caused us even a moment's worry.'

Luc placed his eating utensils down and laid his hands on the table. 'Thackeray led me to believe the girls were being looked after in the manner my late wife would have wished them to be. If I had had any notion of the lack of finance you have put up with for the last God knows how many months—' he stopped as the old lady winced at his profanity '—for the last months,' he repeated, 'then I would have been up here a lot sooner.'

'So we can stay?' Hope asked the question, the same emotion as her name easily heard in her voice.

'Indeed you can, and I will see to it as soon as I return to London.'

He left Woodruff Abbey with all of its inhabitants waving him goodbye and a handful of warm potatoes wrapped in cloth that Charity had given him.

The first thing he did when he arrived in the city was to tell the elderly Horatio Thackeray that his services as his lawyer were no longer needed, and set an investigator on to the trail of finding where the money had gone. In his stead he hired a younger and more compassionate man whose reputation had been steadily rising in the city.

'So you wish for Woodruff Abbey to be kept in trust for the children?' David Kennedy's voice contained a tone in it that could most succinctly be described as incredulous.

'That is correct.'

'You realise of course that once the deed is filed it is binding and you would have no hope of seeing your property back should you change your mind at a later date?'

'I do.'

'You also wish for the monies from the estate to be placed in a fund to see to the running of the Abbey, and for a specified number of servants to be hired to help the older couple?'

'That is right.'

'Then if you are certain that that is what you want and you have understood the finality of such a generous gesture, you must sign here. To begin the process, you understand. I shall get back to you within the month when the deeds are written.'

A quick scrawl and it was done. Luc replaced the ink pen in its pot and gathered his hat.

'There is one proviso, Mr Kennedy.'

The lawyer looked startled.

'The proviso is that you tell no one of this.'

'You do not wish others to know of your generosity?'

'I do not.'

'Very well, sir. Will that be all today?'

'No, there is another thing. I am transferring funds from an account I hold here in London, which shall stay in place in case of any shortfall. Under no circumstance at all do I wish for the inhabitants of the Abbey to go without again. If indeed there is any problem at all, I expect to be contacted with as much haste as you could muster to remedy the matter.'

'That shall be done, sir. Might I also say how pleased I am to have the chance to do business with you—'

'Thank you,' Luc cut him short. He had a card game he could not miss that was due to start in just over two hours and he needed to take the omnibus to Piccadilly.

Lillian tucked her diary away in the small console by her bed and told herself that she should not write of her thoughts of Lucas Clairmont.

She had heard that he had been away from London for the past five days, travelling according to Nathaniel Lindsay's wife, Cassandra, who was the sister of Anne Weatherby. Where, she had no clue, though according to Anne he had left his lodgings and given no idea of when he expected to return.

Presumably it would be before the house party on Friday. She wondered who he knew in England to take him away for such a period and remembered the Countess of Horsham's scandalous gossip. Lillian shook her head. Surely a man of little means and newly come from the Americas would not have the wherewithal to house any children, let alone those born out of wedlock?

Lucas Clairmont was a mystery, she thought, his accent changing each time she saw him and some dark menace in his golden eyes. Not a man to be trifled with, she decided, and not a man whom others might persuade to take any course he did not wish to, either.

She made her way down to the library on the first floor of the town house and dislodged a book on the Americas that her father had bought a few years earlier. Virginia and Hampton and the wide ragged outline of Chesapeake Bay was easily traced by her fingers and there along a blue line signifying the James River lay Richmond, surrounded by green and at the edge of long tongues of water that wound their way up towards it. What hills and dales did he know? What towns to the east and west had he visited? Charlottesville. Arlington. Williamsburg and Hopewell. All names that she had no knowledge of and only the propensity to imagine.

A knock on the door brought her from her reveries and she called an entry.

'Lord Wilcox-Rice is here, ma'am, with his sister, Lady Eleanor. He said something of a shopping expedition.'

'What time is it?' Lillian asked the question in trepidation.

'Half past three, miss. Just turned.'

Rising quickly, she was glad that her day dress was one that would not need changing and pleased, too, for the bright sky she could now see outside.

'Of course. Would you show them through to the blue salon and let them know that I shall be but a moment whilst I fetch my bonnet and coat.'

Ellie Wilcox-Rice was one of Lillian's favourite acquaintances; in fact, it was probably due to her influence that Lillian had allowed even the talk of an engagement to her friend's brother to be mooted.

* * *

As they walked along Park Lane she laughed at Ellie's rendition of her Saturday evening at a ball in Kensington, a wearying sort of affair, it seemed.

'I should have much rather been at the crush of James Cholmondely's ball.' Ellie sighed. 'Jennifer Parker said she had the most wonderful time and that she had danced with an American with whom she fell in love on the spot.'

'Probably Mr Lucas Clairmont,' John said, waiting as the girls looked at a shop window, beautifully decorated for the approaching Christmas season. 'He has all the ladies' hearts a-racing, I hear, and no one has any idea of who exactly he is.'

'Does he have your heart a-racing, Lillian?' Ellie's laughter was shrill.

'Of course he doesn't,' John answered for her. 'Lillian is far too sensible to be swayed by the man.'

'Jennifer thinks he is rich. She thinks he has land in the Americas that rival that of the Ancaster estate. Hundreds and thousands of acres.'

'Did he say so to her?' Lillian was intrigued by this new development.

'No. It is just she has a penchant for Mr Darcy in *Pride and Prejudice* and imagines Lucas Clairmont in much the same mould.'

'A peagoose, then, and more stupid than I had imagined her.' John's outburst was unexpected. Usually he saw the best in all people.

'Jennifer also said that you had a waltz with this man, Lillian.'

'Indeed I did, and he is a competent dancer, if I recall.'

'But he made no impression upon you?'

Looking away, Lillian hated her breathlessness and her racing heart. To even talk of him here…

'Why, speaking of the devil, I do believe that is him coming towards us now. With Lord Hawkhurst, is it not?'

His sister laid her hand upon his. 'John, you absolutely must introduce me to him and let me make up my own mind.'

The two men walked towards them, both tall and dark, though today it appeared as though Luc Clairmont laboured in his gait and when they came up close Lillian could well see why. Today he looked little like he had last time she had met him, his left eye swollen shut and a cut across the bridge of his nose. When her glance flickered to his hands she saw that he wore gloves. To cover the damage to his knuckles, she supposed, and frowned.

'Wilcox-Rice.' Lord Hawkhurst bowed his head and the exchanges of names were made. When it was her turn for introduction, however, Luc Clairmont made no mention of the intimacy of their meetings so far, tipping his hat in much the same way as he did for Eleanor.

Today the light in his one good eye was dulled considerably, his glance almost bashful as she looked upon him. He barely spoke, waiting until Hawkhurst had finished and then moving along with him.

'Well,' said Eleanor as they went out of earshot, 'it looks as if Jennifer's prince has had an accident.'

'Been in another fight, more like it,' John interjected. 'There was talk of a scuffle at the Lenningtons' the other week.'

'Really.' Ellie turned to look back and Lillian wished that she would not.

'Who would he fight?'

'The gambling tables have their own complications.' John was quick to answer his sister's question. 'Your cousin, by the way, Lillian, is numbered amongst those who have had more than a light dab at the faces of others.'

'Daniel?' Ellie questioned, grimacing at the name. 'But he dresses far too well to fight.'

Despite herself Lillian laughed at the sheer absurdity of her friend's statement as they made their way into Oxford Street.

'I can well see why Jennifer Parker is so besotted. Have you ever seen a more dangerous-looking man than Lucas Clairmont?'

When John frowned heavily, they decided that it was prudent to drop the subject altogether.

Christmas decorations were beginning to appear in more of the shops and a child and an elderly woman stood by the roadside selling bunches of mistletoe from a barrow.

Ellie rushed over dragging Lillian with her, carefully separating the foliage until she found a piece that she wanted.

'They say if you kiss a man under mistletoe you will

find your one true love. Wouldn't that be wonderful? Perhaps you might kiss my brother? Here, Lillian, I will buy a sprig for you.'

Eleanor gave the woman some money and was handed two brown parcels, the greenery contained in thick paper and string. As they went to leave a young couple came up to the barrow. They were not well-to-do or dressed in anything near the latest of fashion, but when the man held the mistletoe up to the woman there was something in their eyes that simply transfixed Lillian.

Laughter and warmth and a shining intensity that was bewitching! She saw love in the way their hands brushed close as he handed her the packet and in the breathless smile the woman gave back to him as she received her gift. Only them in the world, only the small circle of their joy and happiness, for the bliss between them was tangible to everyone that watched.

Yearning overcame Lillian. Yearning for what she had just seen, the mistletoe a reminder of what she had never found and would probably never have. She glanced at John, who was castigating his sister for wasting her money on such frippery and a heavy sadness settled over her.

Christmas with its hope and promise had a way of undermining rationality and logic, replacing it with this mistletoe magic and a great dollop of hunger for something completely untenable.

'I do hope you are not swayed by my sister's nonsense, too?' John said, and with the shake of her head

Lillian placed the brown packet in her bag and averted her eyes from the couple now walking on the other side of the street.

Chapter Six

Her cousin Daniel was in the library the next morning when she went down to find again the book on the Americas and he did not look pleased.

'Lillian. It has been a while since we have talked.' His face was marked by the underlying anger she had got used to seeing there.

For the past few years Daniel had been away from England and the ease of conversation that they had at one time had was now replaced by distance. Some other more nebulous wildness was also evident.

'Does my father know that you are here?'

'Yes. He is just retrieving a document that my mother has asked me to find for her.'

'I see.'

He flipped at the pages of the book on America as it lay open on the table next to him. 'It's a big land. I was there on the east coast. Washington, mainly, and New York.'

'Is that where you met Mr Clairmont?'

He frowned and then realisation dawned. 'Ah, you saw us the other night at the Lenningtons'.'

'I met him in the street yesterday with Hawkhurst. He had the appearance of being in another fight and I thought perhaps—' But he did not let her finish!

'Stay away from him, Lillian, for he is trouble.'

She nodded, and, pleased to hear her father's foot-steps in the hall, excused herself.

John Wilcox-Rice arrived alone in the afternoon and he had brought her a bunch of winter cheer. Blooms that would sit well in her room and she thanked him.

Today he was dressed in a dark blue frock coat, brown trousers and a waistcoat of lighter blue. His taste was impeccable, she thought, his Hessians well pol-ished and fashionable.

After her talk with her cousin that morning she was in a mood to just let life take her where it would. Thoughts of children and a home of her own were becoming more formed. Perhaps a life with John would be a lot more than tolerable? Her father liked him, her aunt liked him and she liked his sister very much. The young couple from yes-terday came briefly to mind, but the time between then and now had dulled her sense of yearning, her more normal sensibleness taking precedence.

So when he took her hand in his she did not pull away, but savoured the feeling of gentle warmth.

'We have known each other for a passably long time, Lillian, and I think that if we gave it the chance…'

When she nodded, he looked heartened.

'I have asked your father if I could court you and he has given his permission. Now I need the same permission from you.'

The warning from Daniel and the Countess of Horsham's gossip welled in her mind.

Stay away from Lucas Clairmont. Stay away from trouble.

'It is six weeks until Christmas. Perhaps we could use this time to see if…?' She could not finish. To see what? To see if she felt passion or fervour or frenzy?

When he drew her up with him in response she stood, and when his lips glided across her own she did try to answer him back, did attempt to summon the hope of joy and benefit.

But she felt nothing!

The shock of it hit her and she pulled away, amazed at the singular smile of ardour on John's face.

'I will consider that as a troth, my love, and I will treasure the beauty of it for ever.'

The sound of a maid coming with tea had him moving away and taking his place on a chair opposite her. Yet still he grinned.

A gentleman, a nice man, a good man. And a man whose kisses made her feel nothing.

She lay in bed that night and cried. Cried for her mother and her father and for herself, trapped as she was by rules and rituals and etiquette.

John's fragrant flowers were on the table beside her

bed, but she missed the ugly single orange bloom. Missed its vigour and its irreverence and its unapologetic raw colour. Missed the company of the man who had given it to her.

He had had a wife who had died quite recently according to the gossip. Lord, how had he dealt with that? Badly, by all accounts, as she thought of his gambling and his obvious lack of funds.

Closing her eyes, she brought her hand to her mouth and kissed the back of it as John Wilcox-Rice had kissed her lips today. There was something wrong with the way that he had not moved, the static stillness of the action negating all the emotion that should have been within it.

Lord, she had never in her life been kissed before and so she was hardly an expert, but a part of her brain refused to believe that that was all that it was, all that was whispered about and written of. No, there had to be more to it than what she had felt today, but with Christmas on its way and the honouring of a promise to find a spouse, she was running out of time to be able to truly discover just what it was.

A new and more daring thought struck her suddenly.

Perhaps she could find out? Perhaps if she invited Lucas Clairmont to call and offered him a sum of money for both his service and his silence, she might discover what she did not now know.

To buy a single kiss!

She smiled, imagining such a wild and dangerous

scheme. Of course she could not do that! Lucas Clairmont was hardly a man to bargain with and any trust she
might give him would be sorely misplaced. Or would
it? He had melted into the background at the Lenning-
ton ball and she had heard no gossip of her conversation on the Belgrave Square balcony. Indeed, when she
had seen him in the street yesterday he had barely acknowledged her. But was that from carefulness or just
plain indifference?

She moved her hand and slanted her lips, increasing
the pressure in a way that felt right. A bloom of want
wound thin in her stomach, the warm promise of it
bringing to mind the dangerous American.

Quickly she sat up, hard against the backboard of the
bed, pulling the bedding about her shoulders to try to
keep the cold at bay.

This was her only chance to find out. She had been
in society for nearly eight years and not once in all that
time had she lain here imagining the things she did now
about any man.

Forty-two days until she would give a promise of
eternal obedience and chastity to a man whose kisses
left her with…nothing.

Her teeth worried her top lip as she tried to imagine
the conversation preceding the experiment. It hardly
seemed loyal to tell him of her reaction to John's kiss
and her need to see if others would be the same, and yet
if she did not he might think her wanton. A new thought
struck her. Could men kiss well if they thought that they

were being compared in some way? Would it not dampen a natural tendency?

And how much should she pay him? Would he be offended by fifty pounds or thankful for it? Would he want a hundred if he kissed her twice?

The hours closed in on her, as did the fact that Luc Clairmont would be gone after Christmas. A useful knowledge that, for he would be a temporary embarrassment only, should her whole scheme founder!

The thought of Christmas turned her thoughts in another direction.

Mistletoe!

That was it. If she hung the mistletoe Ellie had bought her yesterday above the doorway and angled herself so that she stood beneath the lintel in front of him... Just an accident, a pleasant interlude that would mean nothing should his kiss rouse as little feeling in her as John's had.

She sat up further.

Would he know of the traditions here in England? Would he even see it?

Could she mention the custom if he did not? Her brain turned this way and that, and the clock in the corner struck the hour of two. Outside the echo of the other clocks lingered.

Did Luc Clairmont hear them too? Was he awake with his swollen eye and wounded leg?

She slipped from her bed and walked to the window, pulling back her heavy cream curtains and looking out into the darkness.

Park Lane was quiet and the trees across the way were bleak against a sodden sky. Tonight the moon did not show its face, but was hidden behind low clouds of rolling greyness, gathering in the west.

A nothing kiss in a rain-filled night and the weight of twenty-five years upon her shoulders.

If she did not take this one chance, she might never know, but always wonder…

Sitting at her desk, she pulled out a piece of paper and an envelope and, dipping her pen in ink, began to write.

The letter had come a few minutes ago and Luc could make no sense of it. Lillian Davenport had something of importance to ask him and would like his company at three o'clock. The servant who had brought the message was one of Stephen's so he presumed it to have gone to the Hawkhurst town house first. The lad also seemed to be waiting for a reply.

Scrawling an answer on a separate sheet of parchment, he reached for his seal. Out of habit, he was to think as he placed it back down, for of course he could not use it here. 'Could you deliver this to Miss Davenport?'

The young servant nodded and hurried away, and when he had gone Luc lifted Lillian's missive into the light and read it again.

She wanted to speak to him about something important. She hoped he would come alone. She wondered about the Christmas traditions in America and whether mistletoe and holly were plants he was familiar with.

He frowned. Though he grew trees for timber in Virginia, the subject of botany had never been his strongpoint. Holly he knew as a prickly red-berried plant but mistletoe… Was that not the sprig that young ladies liked to hang in the Yuletide salons to catch kisses? A different thought struck him. What would it be like to kiss Lillian Davenport?

He chastised himself at the very idea. Lord, she seemed to be very familiar with Wilcox-Rice and he was leaving in little more than a month.

But the thought lingered, a tantalising conjecture that lay in the memory of holding her fingers in his own and feeling the hurried beat of her heart. He guessed that Lillian Davenport was a warm and responsive woman beneath the outward composure, a lady who would be pleasantly surprised by the wonders of the flesh.

Raking his hand through his hair, he stood, wincing at the lump on the back of his head. Four men had jumped him on returning to his lodgings three nights ago and it was only his training in the army that had allowed him the ability to fend them off until help arrived.

He wished that Hawk had not persuaded him to take a walk the other day, the same walk that had brought him face to face with Lillian and her friends. Damn, he had seen in her eyes the censure he had noticed in every single one of their meetings and who could blame her?

The charade of his visit here began to press in. He would have liked to tell Lillian that he was not a bad man, that he had been a soldier and that he held great tracks of virgin land in Virginia filled with timber. But he couldn't because there were other things about him that she would not countenance.

Still, for the first time in a long while he felt alive and excited, the inertia in Richmond replaced by a new vigour.

He came through into the small yellow downstairs salon like one of the sleek black panthers she had once seen as a statue in an antique shop in Regent Street, all restless energy and barely harnessed menace, but she also saw he limped.

'Miss Davenport!' Today his injured eye looked darker, the bruising worsened by time, though he neither alluded to it nor hid it from her. Her letter was in his hand, she could see her tidy neat writing from where she stood and there was a question in his stance.

'Mr Clairmont.'

Silence stretched until she gestured him to sit, the absurdity of all she had planned, now that he was here, screaming in her consciousness. How did she begin? How did one broach such a situation with any degree of modesty and honour?

'Thank you very much for coming. I know that you must be busy—'

'Card games happen mostly at night,' he interrupted and she swore she saw a glimmer of amusement in his velvet eyes.

'And your leg is obviously painful,' she hurried on. To that he stayed wordless.

Her eyes strayed to the door. Did she risk broaching the subject before the parlourmaid brought in the refreshments or after? Relaxing, she decided on after, reasoning she could then instruct the girl to leave them alone for the few moments it would take to conduct her…experiment.

Lord, she hated to call it that, but was at a loss as to what else to name it.

'I hope London is treating you well…' As soon as she said it she knew her error.

'A few cuts and bruises, but what is that between a man and a beautiful city?'

'Was it a fall?'

He frowned at that and grated out a 'yes'.

'I had an accident last year at Fairley, our family seat in Hertfordshire.'

'Indeed?' His brows rose significantly.

'I fell from a horse whilst racing across the park.'

'I trust nothing was broken?'

'Only my pride! It was a village fair, you see, and I had entered the race on a whim.'

'Pride is a fragile thing,' he returned in his American drawl, and her cheeks reddened. She shifted in her seat, hating the heat that followed and fretful that her letter had indeed told him far too much. Her eyes flickered to the mistletoe she had hung secretly, a sad reminder of a plot that was quickly unravelling, and then back to his hands lying palm up in his lap.

Suddenly she knew just how to handle her request. 'You told me once of a woman who had read your hand in the town of Richmond?'

She waited till he nodded.

'You said that she told you life was like a river and that you are taken by it to the place that you were meant to be.' The tone of her voice rose and she fought to keep it back.

'The thing is, Mr Clairmont, I would hope at this moment that the place you are meant to be is here in my salon because I am going to ask you a question that might, without some sense of belief in fate, sound strange.'

'I know very little about the properties of mistletoe or holly,' he interrupted. 'If it is botany that you wish to quiz me on?'

'I beg your pardon?'

'Your letter. You mention something of particular plants.'

Unexpectedly she began to smile and then caught the mirth back with a strong will as she shook her head.

'No, it is not that. I had heard from…others that the state of your finances is somewhat precarious and wanted to offer you a boon to alleviate the problem.' She knew that she had taken the wrong turn as soon as he stood, the polite façade of a moment ago submerged beneath anger.

Panic made her careless. 'I want to buy a kiss from you.' Blurted out with all the finesse of a ten-year-old.

'You what…?'

'Buy a kiss from you…' Her hands shook as she

rummaged through her bag, trying to extricate the notes she had got from the bank that very morning.

When she finally managed it he swore, and not quietly.

'Shh, they might hear.'

'Who might hear? Your father? Your cousin? Someone has already had one go at me this week and I would be loathe to let them have another one.'

'Someone did that to you?' Goodness, she had lost hold of the whole conversation and could not even think how to retrieve it.

With honesty!

Taking a breath, she buried vanity. 'I am a twenty-five-year-old spinster, Mr Clairmont, and a woman who has been kissed only once, yesterday, by Lord Wilcox-Rice. And I need to know if what I felt was... normal.'

'What the hell did you feel?'

She drew herself up to her tallest height, a feat that was not so intimidating given that she stood at merely five foot two, even in her shoes.

'I felt nothing!'

The words reverberated in the ensuing silence, his anger evaporating in an instant to be replaced by laughter.

'I realise to you that the whole thing may seem like a joke, but...'

He breathed out. Hard.

'Nay, it is not that, Lilly, it is not that.' She felt his hand against her cheek, a single finger stroking down the bone, a careful feather-touch with all the weight of air.

A touch that made her shiver and want, a touch that made her move towards this thing she wished for, and then vanishing as a sound came from outside in the corridor.

Luc Clairmont moved back too, towards the window, his body faced away from hers and his hand adjusting the fit of his trousers. Perhaps he was angry again? Perhaps on reflection he saw the complete and utter disregard of convention that her request had subjected him to?

She smiled wanly as a young maid entered the room and bade her leave the tea for them to pour. Question shadowed the girl's eyes and Lillian knew that she was fast running out of minutes. It was simply not done for an unmarried lady to be sequestered alone for any length of time with a man.

At twenty-five some leeway might have been allowed, but she knew that he would need to leave before too many more seconds had passed.

Consequently when the door shut behind the servant she walked across to him.

'I do not wish to hurry you, but—'

He did not let her finish. The hard ardour of his lips slanted across her own, opening her mouth. Rough hands framed her cheeks as the length of his body pressed against hers, asking, needing, allowing no mealy response, but the one given from the place she had hidden for so, so long.

Feeling exploded, the sharp beat of her heart, the

growing warmth in her stomach, the throb of lust that ached in a region lower. As she pressed closer her hands threaded through his hair, and into the nape of his neck, moving without her volition, with a complete lack of control.

He was not gentle, not careful, the feel of his lips on her mouth, on her cheek and on the sensitive skin at her neck unrestrained.

And then stopped!

She tried to keep it going, tipping her mouth to his, but he pulled her head against his chest and held her there, against a heartbeat that sped in heavy rhythm.

'This is not the place, Lilly…'

Reality returned, the yellow salon once again around her, the sound of servants outside, the tea on the table with its small plume of steam waiting to be drunk.

She pushed away, a new danger now in the room and much more potent than the one that had bothered her before.

Before she had been worried about his actions and now she was worried about her own, for in that kiss something had been unleashed, some wild freedom that could now not be contained.

Lucas Clairmont placed her letter on the table and gathered his hat. 'Miss Davenport,' he said and walked from the room.

Lord, he thought on the journey between Pall Mall and his lodgings. He should not have kissed her, not allowed her confession of feeling 'nothing' with Wilcox-Rice to sway his resolve.

And now where did it leave him? With a hankering for more and a woman who would hate him.

He should have stayed, should have reassured her, should have at least had the decency to admit the whole thing as his fault before he had walked out.

But she had captivated him with her pale elegance and honesty and with the fumbled bank notes pushed uncertainly at him.

To even think that she would pay him?

Absolute incredulity replaced irritation and that in turn was replaced by something…more akin to respect.

She was the one all others aspired to be like, the pinnacle of manners and deportment and it could not have been easy for her to have even asked him what she did. Hell, she had a hundred times more to lose than he, with his passage to Virginia looming near and a reputation that no amount of bad behaviour could lower.

Why on earth, then, had she picked him? She must have weighed up the odds as to what he could do with such information, the pressures of society here like a sledgehammer against any deviation from the strict codes of manners.

Why had she risked it?

The answer came easily. She did so because she was desperate, desperate to discover if what she felt for Wilcox-Rice was normal and hopeful that it was not.

Well, he thought, with the first glimmer of humour coming back. At least she had found out that!

Lillian threw herself on her bed and took the breath she had hardly taken since Lucas Clairmont had left the house.

He had been angry, the notes she had tried to give him in her fist, a coarse message of intent and failure. She rolled over and peeled each one away from the other.

Two hundred pounds! And if he had taken them it would have been worth every single penny. Turning, she looked at the ceiling, reliving each second of that kiss, her fingers reaching for the places his had been and then falling lower.

What if he had not stopped? What if he had not pulled back when he did? Would she have come to her senses? Honesty forced her to admit she would not have and the admission cost her much.

'If you aren't careful you will be your mother all over again, Lillian.' Her father's voice from the past, a warning to her as her mother lay dying, the words uttered in a despair of melancholy and sorrow. She had been thirteen and the fashions of the day had begun to be appealing, the chance to experiment and change. She blinked.

Had such advice altered the person she might have become? Was she changing back?

She shook her head and lay still, closing her eyes against the light.

* * *

The knock on the door woke her and for a second she could not work out quite where she was, for seldom did she doze in the afternoon.

Her bedroom. Lucas Clairmont. The kiss. Reality surfaced and with it a rising dread.

'You have some flowers, Miss.'

A maid came in with a large unruly bunch of orange flowers and her breath was caught. 'Is there a card?'

'Indeed, miss, there is.' The maid broke the envelope away from a string that kept it joined to the bouquet, speculation unhidden in the lines of her face.

'That will be all, thank you,' Lillian said, waiting until the door was shut before she slit open the card.

I FELT SOMETHING

The words were in bold capitals with no name attached.

Without meaning to, Lillian began to cry—in those three words Luc Clairmont had given her back the one thing she had not thought it possible to regain.

Her pride.

Holding the flowers close to her breast, her tears fell freely across the fragrant orange petals.

Chapter Seven

'Mr Clairmont from America was at the club as a guest of Hawkhurst today.' The tone in her father's voice told her that he was not pleased. 'The man is a scoundrel and a gambler. Why he even continues to receive invitation from people we know confounds me.'

'And yet he seemed such a nice young man when he came to ask you to dance, Lillian, at the Cholmondely ball. How very misleading first impressions can be,' her aunt said.

'You have danced with this American?' Her father's heavy frown made her heart sink.

Danced. Touched. Kissed.

'I have, Father. He asked for my hand in a waltz.'

'And you did not turn him down? Surely you could see what sort of a fellow he was.'

'Men like him pounce quickly on the unsuspecting,

Ernest. It is no point in chastising Lillian, for she is blameless in it all.'

Blameless?

The bunch of orange blooms still stood by her bed, carefully tended and watered daily, but she had not seen him again, not in the park, not at the parties, not in the streets as she walked each day.

'St Auburn is a particular friend of Clairmont's, is he not?'

Jean shrugged her shoulders. 'I do not know the man personally. Daniel could probably tell you much more about him.'

Lillian looked more closely at her aunt, trying to ascertain whether she knew of the wayward pursuits of her son and deciding in the smile she returned her that she probably did not.

'I ask the question,' her father continued, 'because an invitation came for you yesterday, Lillian, to attend a country party of the Earl and Lady St Auburn in Kent and I should not wish for you to go should the American be there.' He sipped at his tea, fiddling with a pair of spectacles he held in his right hand.

'When would the party be held, Father?' She tried to keep her voice as neutral as she could.

'It would run from this Friday to Sunday. If you were interested, perhaps Wilcox-Rice could take you?'

'Indeed.' She bit into her toast and honey.

'So you are saying that you would go?'

'Lady St Auburn is a friend of mine. I should like to catch up with her news.'

'Would you be able to travel down too, Jean? Lillian can hardly go unchaperoned.'

Her aunt sighed heavily, but accepted the responsibility, giving the impression of a woman who would have preferred to be saying no.

The house was beautiful, a six-columned Georgian mansion, the grounds as well manicured and fine as she had visited anywhere.

They were late. She could see that as they swept up the circular driveway, a crowd of people in a glass conservatory to the left of the house. From this distance she could not be sure that Lucas Clairmont was amongst them, but John Wilcox-Rice at her side did not look happy.

'I cannot imagine why you should want to come to this party, Lillian. The set St Auburn hangs with are a little wild and if he did not have so much in the way of property and gold I doubt he would be so feted. Besides, the man always seems slightly unrestrained to me.'

'Cassandra is Mrs Weatherby's youngest sister, John, and I have a lot of fondness for her.'

'Then you should have seen her in the city.'

'But Kent is lovely at this time of the year. Surely you would at least say that?'

Jean stretched suddenly, waking as the carriage slowed and stopped.

'Goodness. Are we here already? The roads south get quicker and quicker. Perhaps we should persuade your father to acquire a property here rather than in Hertfordshire, Lillian, for it is so much more convenient for London.' She looked out of the window at the sky. 'Have you ever seen such a clear horizon, none of the yellow smog on show?'

A group of servants milled around the coach, waiting for the party to alight, the younger boys already hauling the luggage off and listening for instructions as to where it should be taken.

The Davenport family seat of Fairley Manor came to Lillian's mind as she saw the precision and order that accompanied their arrival. The housekeeper bowed and presented herself and the head butler was most attentive to any needs that the small group might have.

Wilcox-Rice in particular was rather grumpy, barely acknowledging the efforts of the St Auburn servants to please. He did not even want to be here, he mumbled under his breath, and Lilly wondered why she had not seen this rather irritating trait in his nature before.

But with the sun in her face and the promise of a whole weekend before her, she felt buoyed up with hope. She had pressed one of her orange flowers in a book in her travel bag to be able to show Lucas Clairmont, for she knew flowers in this season would have cost him a fortune that he did not possess and she wanted him to know, at least, that she had appreciated the gesture.

'Lillian!' Her name was called and she turned to see who summoned her. Cassandra St Auburn walked towards her, her bright red hair aflame and the sweetness in her face all that Lillian remembered.

'You came! I thought perhaps that you would not.'

'Indeed, it is such a lovely spot I should be loathe to miss out. Lady St Auburn, this is Lord Wilcox-Rice. It was noted on my invitation that I could bring a partner.'

'Yes, of course.' Cassie shook the outstretched hand and Lillian detected disquiet. 'But I thought your aunt was coming…'

'Here I am, my dear, a little late to alight, but the bones are not quite as they used to be.' Jean thanked the servant who had helped her and turned to the house. 'I was here when I was about your age with Leonard St Auburn.'

'My husband's grandfather. He is still here, though he spends much of his day now in the library.'

'A well-read man, if I remember rightly. Very interested in the world of plants.'

Cassandra laughed and Lillian liked the sound. A happy and uncomplicated girl! Sometimes she wished she could have been more like that.

'Most of the party are in the conservatory,' she continued on. 'Would you join us there after you refresh yourselves?'

'That would be lovely,' Lillian answered as they were ushered inside, the quickened beat of her heart steadying a little as they mounted the staircase.

Twenty minutes later they walked towards the group of guests standing around a table well stocked with food and drink.

Lucas Clairmont was nowhere in sight and part of her was annoyed that she could not have met him here informally. The Earl of St Auburn, Nathaniel, came over to join his wife. He had once rather liked her, Lillian recalled, when she had first come out, though it was such a long time ago she doubted he would remember it.

'Miss Davenport!' His smile was welcoming. 'And Lord Wilcox-Rice.' Her Aunt Jean had elected not to come downstairs, but have a rest so that she would be refreshed for dinner. 'We are very pleased that you could both make the journey.'

He placed a strange emphasis on 'both' and Lillian saw a quick frown pass between the St Auburns, an unspoken warning from Cassandra, she thought were she to interpret it further. Did they already perceive her and John as a couple? She swallowed back worry.

'You have a large number of people here. Do you expect any more?' Her mind raced. If Lucas Clairmont did not come after sending her the invitation she would never forgive him!

'A few of the neighbours will come tonight for dinner and Mr Clairmont will bring Lady Shelby down from London.'

'Caroline Shelby?' John's voice had the same ring of masculine appreciation that she had heard in the tone of each man who had discussed the newest beauty on the London scene.

'She couldn't leave town any earlier so Nat asked his friend to wait and escort her.'

Lillian felt the muscles in her cheeks shake, so tight did she try to hold her smile. If Clairmont had invited her here to flirt in front of someone else… Lord, the whole weekend would be untenable and she wondered how she might return to London without causing conjecture.

No. Her resolve firmed—she would not turn tail and disappear. For five days now she had been walking on eggshells at every single social occasion just in case she should see him, her words rehearsed so as to deliver the nonchalant greeting she wanted.

She needed to thank him for the flowers and move on to the next part of her life, and if memory served her well she knew him to be off to America in merely a few weeks' time.

Luc waited as the girl gathered her shawl and minced to the carriage. Her chaperon, a woman in her mid-forties, followed behind her. Lord, would they ever be ready to go? He looked at his watch and determined that Lillian Davenport should have already arrived in Kent.

Would Nathaniel have told her of the reason for his lateness?

Caroline Shelby placed her hand in his as she gained the carriage steps and kept it there long after the need lapsed. Extracting his fingers, he put his hands firmly by his side, sitting on the seat opposite from the two women and looking out of the window.

'It should take an hour,' he said with as little emotion as he could muster.

Caroline giggled, the sound filling the carriage. 'They say the St Auburns have a beautiful house?'

'Indeed they do.'

'They say if you rode from one end of the estate to the other it may take all of a day.'

'It may.'

The echo of Virginia loomed large. To go from one end of his property to the other would take a week and he missed it with an ache that surprised him.

'I should love to see it on horseback. Do you ride?'

He nodded, hoping she did not see this affirmation as an invitation.

'Then we must find some horses and venture out,' she replied and his heart sank at the sentence.

'I have some business with the Earl—' he began but she interrupted him.

'But you could find an hour or so for a lady who has asked you?' Her hand closed over his and the chaperon looked away.

'Certainly.' Luc resolved to make a large party of this sojourn even as he removed his fingers yet again from hers.

Forty-eight long minutes later the St Auburns' country seat came into view and the woman who sat next to Lady Shelby finally seemed to deem it time to haul the antics of her young charge in.

'Your hat is a little crooked, dear,' she said, deft

fingers straightening the bonnet that had come askew when she had fallen forwards against him on one of the more rutted sections of the road. 'And you really ought to replace your gloves.'

The sight of the house as they swept on to the circular drive was welcome and it seemed as if many of the houseguests still languished in the glassed-in conservatory, enjoying the last rays of the sun. He easily picked out Lillian, her pale hair entwined today into one single bunch, simple and elegant and the white gown complimenting her figure. She had not seen him, but was talking to Cassandra and next to her stood…John Wilcox-Rice.

'Damn.' He swore beneath his breath, glad for the chance to vacate the carriage and escape the company of the irritating Lady Shelby and her dour chaperon.

Nathaniel met him first. 'Wilcox-Rice is here.' A warning flinted strong.

'I saw him.'

'Should I stand between you?'

'To keep the peace, you mean?'

'He is rumoured to have offered for her hand. If you mean to pursue that gleam I can see in your eyes…'

'Have patience, Nat. Any protection that you feel the need to give me will be relinquished in a few weeks.'

'You think that you'll be on that boat?' A strange smile filled the eyes of his friend.

'Of course I will be. My passage is booked and paid for. There is nothing to hold me here.'

'Or no one?'

Luc laughed suddenly, seeing where it was Nathaniel was going with this line of question. 'I tried marriage once.' His words were bleak and he hated the tightness in them.

'Elizabeth was a woman who would drive anyone to the bottle. God knows why you still wear her damn ring.'

Luc felt a singular shot of fury consume him. 'I wear it because it reminds me.'

'Reminds you of what?'

'Never to make the same mistake twice.' He grabbed a drink of fruit punch from the table as he moved away.

Lillian turned as Lucas Clairmont downed a large glass of punch, the lot hardly touching his throat before he helped himself to another.

He looked angry and she could not quite reconcile this man with the one who had sent her flowers and kept silent about a scandal that could easily ruin her. The bruising around his eye was largely gone and the velvet of his dangerous glance made her wary and uncertain. Caroline Shelby seemed bent on following him and Lillian could well see why she had been often named as the most beautiful girl of her Season. Wilcox-Rice beside her laid his hand beneath Lillian's elbow in a singular message of claim and she saw Clairmont take in the movement.

Caught between convention and other people's expectations, she could do nothing save for smile, her practised speech of thanks buried under the weight of a careful control.

'Miss Davenport.' When she gave him her hand he held it briefly. The warmth of his skin made her start with the recognition of his touch.

'Mr Clairmont. It is nice to see you once again.'

He dropped contact almost immediately.

'You two know each other?' Cassandra was astonished.

'A little.' Her words.

'Not well.' His.

Cassie's giggles drew the attention of Caroline Shelby as she gained their small circle.

'What a lovely party! I knew I should have left London earlier. If it had not been for you, Mr Clairmont, I should not even be here by now. I hope that I have not missed too much, for you all seem very festive.'

'I am certain you are quite in time, Lady Shelby,' Lillian returned.

'Miss Davenport. How wonderful that you should be here. I have long admired your sense of style and bearing and your dress—' she gestured to the white moiré silk '—why, it is just so beautiful.'

'Thank you.'

'My friend Eloise says you have your clothes made in England, but I think that cannot be true as the cut and cloth is just too wonderful and I said to my mother the other day that we should ask you about your seamstress and use her ourselves because…'

Was she nervous, Lillian thought, switching out of the constant barrage of never-ending chatter, or just frivolous? She made the mistake of glancing at Lucas

Clairmont and almost laughed at the comical disbelief on his face. Lord, and he had had a whole hour of it coming down from London. No wonder he had almost leapt from the coach as soon as it had stopped.

'Do you enjoy flowers, Miss Davenport?' Caroline's shrill and final question pierced her ruminations.

'I do indeed.'

'Is not the garden here just beautiful? All in shades of white, too. I suppose with your penchant for the paler hues you would prefer your flowers in the same sort of palette?'

Lillian smiled. Now here was an opening she could take, and easily. 'Lately I find that I have a growing preference for orange.'

She caught the expression of puzzlement on Lucas Clairmont's face, but with John at her side could make no further comment.

'Orange?' The girl opposite almost shouted the word. 'Oh, no, Miss Davenport, surely you jest with me?'

When Cassandra St Auburn suggested that the party now retire to dress for dinner Lillian could do nothing but lift her skirts and follow, noticing with chagrin that Lucas Clairmont did not join them.

Chapter Eight

Luc took a sixteen-hand gelding from the stables of St Auburn and rode for Maygate, a village a good ten miles away. He was tired and using the last light of dusk and the first slice of moon to guide him he journeyed west.

Dinner would still be a few hours away and he felt the need to stretch his body and feel the wind on his face and freedom.

Lord, how the English enjoyed their long and complicated afternoon teas, something which in Virginia would have been thought of as ludicrous.

Virginia and a green tract of land that reached from the James to the Potomac. His land! Hewed from the blood, sweat and tears of hard labour, the timber within his first hundred acres bringing the riches to buy the rest.

A piecemeal acquisition!

He ran his thumb across the scar on his thigh, feeling the ridges of flesh badly healed. An accident when the Bank of Washington was about to foreclose on him and he had no other means of paying to get the wood out. He had dragged it alone along the James by horse, unseated as a log rose across another and his mount bolted, pushing him into the jagged end of newly hewn timber. The cut had festered badly, but still he had made it to Hopewell and the mill that would buy the load, staving off the greed of the bank for a few more months.

Hard days. Lonely days.

Not as lonely as when Elizabeth had come, though, with her needs and wants and sadness.

No, he would not think of any of that, not here, not in the mellow countryside of Kent where the boundaries of safety were a comfortable illusion.

'Lately I find I have a growing preference for orange.' The words drifted to him from nowhere, warming him with possibility. Was it the flowers he had given her she spoke of? He shook his head. Better for Lillian Davenport to marry Wilcox-Rice than him and have the promise of an English heritage that was easy and prudent.

He stopped in a position overlooking a stream, the shadows of night long as he ran his fingers through his hair. Such dreams were no longer for him and he had been foolish to even think they could be. He should depart again tonight for London, leaving Lilly with her enticing full lips and woman's body to his imagination. But he could not. Already he found himself turning his horse for home.

* * *

Lillian felt like a young girl again, this dress not quite fitting and that one not quite right. She was glad for the help of her lady's maid and glad too that her aunt Jean was still in bed, her headache having turned into a cold.

When she finally settled on a gown she liked she walked to the window and looked out. The last of the daylight was lost, the moon rising quickly in the eastern sky and the gardens of St Auburn wreathed in shadow. She was about to turn away when a lone rider caught her eye, his gait on the horse fluid. No Sunday rider this, the beat of the hooves fast and furious.

Lucas Clairmont. She knew it was him, the raw power of his thighs wrapped about the steed in easy control and the reins caught only lightly as the animal held its head and thundered on to the gravelled circle of the driveway.

Caught in the moonlight, hair streaming almost to his shoulders and without a jacket, he looked to her like the living embodiment of some ancient Grecian God. What would it be like to lie with such a man, to feel him near her, close?

Shocked, she turned away. Ladies did not ponder such fantasies and she had been warned many times of the man that he was. Yet surely a light flirtation was a harmless thing and, perhaps, if she were generous, she could place her clandestinely bought kiss into that category. But she should take it no further. To cross the line from coquetry into blowsy abandonment would be to throw away everything that she had worked hard for all her life. Stepping to the mirror, she looked at herself honestly, observed eyes full of anticipation and the smile that seemed to crouch there, waiting.

For him!

Adjusting her chemise so that a little more flesh than usual was showing, she smiled, still proper indeed, but bordering on something that was not. This wickedness that had leaked into her refined formality was freeing somehow, a part of her personality that had until lately lain dormant and unrealised.

'Oh God, please help me.' Spoken into the silence of her room, she wondered just exactly what it was that she was asking. For absolution of sin or for the strength to see her virtue in the way she had always tried to view it? Shaking her head, she sought for the words to cancel such a selfish prayer and found that she couldn't. There was some impunity received, after all, in asking for celestial help and a sense of providence. Tonight she would need both.

Proceeding in to dinner on the arm of the Earl of St Auburn, Lillian was surprised when Clairmont found his seat next to hers. Status and rank almost always determined seating after the formal promenade and she was astonished to see John consigned to a place at the other end of the table and looking most displeased. Cassandra St Auburn raised her glass and Lillian wondered at the definitive twinkle in the woman's glance. Had she planned this? Was there some communal strategy behind the reason for her invitation? Well, she thought, the usual nerve-racking worry of seating seemed to have been done away with completely and the lack of any remorse was, if anything, refreshing.

At her own dinner parties the seating arrangements were what she always hated the most in her fear of offending some personage of higher status than the next one.

Determining to think no more of it, she took a quick peek at the American. His hair was slicked back tonight, still wet from a late bath she supposed after the exercise that he had taken.

'I saw you return from your ride.' She spoke because she found the growing silence between them unnerving.

'After the carriage trip I needed to blow away the cobwebs.' A loud trill from Caroline Shelby two places away punctuated his words. 'Need I say more?' He smiled as she looked shocked. 'It must be difficult to always be so virtuous, Miss Davenport.'

'I am hardly that, Mr Clairmont.' The kiss they had shared quivered between them, an unspoken shout. 'You of all people should know it.'

'Your small experiment to…determine emotion can hardly be consigned to the "fallen woman" basket. Nay, put it down instead to any adult's healthy pursuit of knowledge.'

He was more honourable in his dismissal of her lapse than he needed to be and a great wave of relief covered her. With shaking hands she took small sips of her wine and then laced her fingers tightly together.

'I thank you for such a congenial summary, but my actions the other day were much less than what I usually expect from myself.'

'As a dubious consolation I can tell you that the wisdom of age dims such exacting standards. When you are as old as I am you will realise the freedom of doing just as one wills.'

'Like fighting with my cousin at the Lenningtons'?'

'Or sending a beautiful woman flowers.'

She was silent, the last rejoinder putting a halt to her fault-finding. *Beautiful.* He thought her that?

'How old are you, Mr Clairmont?' She hated herself for asking the question in the face of everything that had passed between them.

'Thirty-three and judicious beyond my years, Miss Davenport.'

'Some here might call you a gambler?'

'Which I am.'

'And a cheat?'

'Which I am not.'

'There are even rumours circulating that hint at the possibility that you have killed people.'

'More than one?' His eyebrows rose in a parody of an actor on the stage, though when she pulled back he laughed. '*"A man can smile and smile and be a villain,"*' he quoted, a new wickedness supplanting the guile.

'You are a puzzle, Mr Clairmont. Just when I think to understand your character you surprise me.'

'With my knowledge of Shakespeare?'

She shook her head. 'Nay, with your intuition on the very nature of mystery!'

'I've had years of practice.'

'And years of debauchery?'

Again he laughed, though this time the sound was less feigned. 'Mirrors and smoke are not solely the domain of the stage, Lilly.'

'Miss Davenport,' she corrected him. 'So are you telling me that what I see is not who you are?'

He tilted his drink up to the light. 'Does not everyone have a hidden side?'

The chatter around her seemed to melt into nothingness and it was as if they were alone, just her and just him, the recognition of want making her feel almost dizzy. Clutching at her seat, she turned away, the room spinning strangely and her heartbeat much too fast.

She was pleased when a delicate pheasant soup was placed before them as it gave her a chance to pretend concentration on something other than Luc Clairmont, and the turbot with lobster and Dutch sauces that followed were delicious.

Lady Hammond, a strong-looking older woman sitting opposite, regaled them on the merits of the hunting in the shire of Somerset as the entrée and removes were served, and by the time the third course of snipes, golden plovers and wild duck came out the topic seemed to have moved on to the wealth and business advantages available in the colonies.

*   *   *

'How do you see it, Mr Clairmont?' one of the older guests asked him. 'How do you see the opportunities in the area around Baltimore and Chesapeake Bay?'

'Men with a little money and fewer morals can do very well there. My uncle's land, for example, was swindled for a pittance and sold for a fortune.'

'By fellow Americans?'

'Nay, by an Englishman. The new industries are profitable and competition is rife.'

The sentence bought a flurry of interest from those around the table and John Wilcox-Rice was quick to add in his penny's-worth. 'It seems that the fibre of our society is threatened by a new generation of youth without morals.'

The Earl of Marling seconded him. 'Integrity and honour come from breeding, and the great families are being whittled away by men who have money, but nothing else.'

Looking down at Luc Clairmont's hand between them, Lillian noticed his knuckles were almost white where he gripped the seat of his chair. Not as nonchalant of it all as his face might show.

Wondering at his manner she was distracted only when a crashing sound made her turn! Lord Paget was drunk and his wife was trying to settle him down again in his seat, the shards from a broken glass spilling from the goblet to the tablecloth and dribbling straight into the lap of John Wilcox-Rice.

Pushing his seat back, John tried to wipe away the damage and Paget in his stupor also reached over to help him, his fingers touching parts that Wilcox-Rice was more than obviously embarrassed by. The tussle that ensued knocked the first man into a second and the tablecloth was partly dragged away from the table, bringing food and wine crashing all around them.

Luc Clairmont was on his feet now as Paget went for Wilcox-Rice.

'Enough,' he said simply, pulling the offender back and blocking an ill-timed punch. 'You are drunk. If you leave with your wife now there will be little damage come morning.'

Paget's wife looked furious, both at her husband's poor behaviour and at Luc Clairmont's interference, but it was Paget who retaliated.

'Perhaps you should be getting your own house into order, Clairmont, before casting aspersions on to ours. You were, after all, expelled from Eton and many would say that you still haven't learned your lesson.'

'Would they now?' His drawl was cold and measured, the gold of his eyes tonight brittle.

'Leave him, my dear, for he is not worth it. If St Auburn wishes to make himself a laughing-stock by insisting the American is a gentleman, then let him.' Lady Paget seemed to be supporting the stupidity of her husband, no thanks being given for the assistance she had received from the man she now railed against.

Anger seized Lillian.

'I would say, Lady Paget, that your manners are far less exacting than the one you would pillory. From where I sit it seems that Mr Clairmont was only trying to make certain that Lord Paget's flagrant lack of etiquette did not harm any of the other ladies present. I for one am very glad that he intervened, as your husband's behaviour was both frightening and unnecessary.'

With a haughty stare she looked about the table, glad when the nods of the others present seemed to support her assessment. Sometimes her position as the queen of manners was an easy crown to wear and a persuasive one. She felt the anger swaying back to the Pagets and away from Luc Clairmont as the wife picked up the heaviness of her skirts and followed her husband, an angry discourse between them distinctly heard.

Lillian did not look around at Lucas Clairmont or question his silence. Nay, she was a woman who knew that if you left people to think too much about a problem then you invariably had a larger one. Consequently she swallowed back ire and began on a topic that she knew would surely interest all the ladies present.

Luc sat next to her and hated the anger that the Pagets' stupid comments had engendered in him. England was the only place in the world, he thought, where the deeds of the past were never forgotten nor forgiven, and where misdemeanours could crawl back into the conversation almost twenty years on.

For now, though, Lilly was chattering on forever

about dresses she had seen in Paris in the summer, and if he had not been so furious he might have admired her attention in remembering the detail of such an unimportant thing.

Not to the women present, however! Each one of them was drinking in her every word and as the servants scooped away shards of china and crystal, replacing the broken with the whole, it was as if there had never been a contretemps. When the dessert of preserved cherries, figs and ginger ice-cream arrived, he noticed that everyone took a generous portion.

Warmth began to spread through him. Lillian Davenport had stood up for him in front of them all, had come to his aid like an avenging angel, her good sense and fine bearing easily persuading everyone of the poor judgement the Pagets had shown.

Indeed, she was lethal, a pale and proper thunderbolt with just the right amount of ire and refinement.

No one could criticise her or slate her decorum and it was with this thought that her offered kiss was even the more remarkable. Lord, did she not realise how easily she could fall, how the inherent nature of man would make any mishap or misconduct accountable in one so loftily placed?

He worried for her, for her goodness and her vulnerability and for the sheer effort that it must take to stay at the very top.

This weekend had been his doing, his own need to see her alone and overriding every other consideration for her welfare. And she had repaid this selfishness with dignity and assurance.

Respect vied with lust and won out. He would do nothing else to bring her reputation into disrepute. That much he promised himself.

He had not come near her since the Pagets had left, the tea taken in the front salon a sedate and formal sort of an affair, with Lucas Clairmont placing himself on the sofa the furthest away from where she sat.

Indeed, after her outburst she thought he might have been a little thankful, but he made no effort at all to converse or even look at her, giving his attention instead to Caroline Shelby and her simpering friend.

Nathaniel St Auburn at her side turned to her to speak. 'I see you had much to talk about with Mr Clairmont earlier on, Miss Davenport?' St Auburn's question was asked in a tone indicating manners rather than inquisitiveness. 'He was an old school friend of mine at Eton,' he enlarged when he saw her surprise. Lillian pondered the thought.

'I didn't realise that he once lived in England.' The cameo of a younger Lucas Clairmont intriguing her. 'He seems too…American?'

Nathaniel chuckled, but there was something in the sound that made her think. She pressed on.

'Have you ever visited him in Virginia?'

'I have.'

'And you enjoyed it?'

'I did!'

Lillian grated her teeth, wishing that his answers might be enlarged so as to give her an insight into the personality of the man sitting across the room from her.

'Mr Clairmont says his home is near a river. The James, I think he said. Does he have family there?' She hoped that the interest she could hear in her words was not so obvious to him.

'His wife was from those parts, but she died in a carriage accident. A nasty thing that, because Luc blamed himself, as any gentleman of sensitivity might.'

Relief bloomed at Luc Clairmont's innocence in his wife's demise. After all the darker conjectures in society, Lillian was pleased to find out that the cause of the woman's death had been an accident, though she had a strange feeling that St Auburn's words were carefully chosen. In warning or in explanation? She could not tell which.

'So you think him a sensitive man?'

'Indeed I do, but I can see by your frown that you may not?'

'I have heard things…'

He did not let her finish. 'Give him a chance,' he said softly and she almost thought that she hadn't heard it before he turned away.

Give him a chance! Of what? She felt again the warmth of Lucas Clairmont's arm against hers where they had not quite touched at the dinner table. If she had moved closer she might have felt him truly, but she had not been brave enough to try. Not there, not then, not with such hooded enquiry seen in so many eyes.

Lord, she seldom came to these country weekend parties and knew now again why she did not. She was stuck here at least till the morrow, any means of escape dubious with her aunt in tow.

John next to her interrupted, making his displeasure known. 'Surely you can see, Lillian, just how the sort of outburst you gave at dinner is damaging? Far wiser indeed to let these small spats run their course and stay well out of it.'

'Even if I should perceive the criticism unfair?' she returned. His social mannerisms were becoming more and more annoying tonight with every new piece of advice that he offered her.

'You are a lady of breeding and cultivation. It is not seemly to be defending a man who has neither.'

'Paget was hardly in order.'

'He was not expelled from Eton for stealing either.'

'Stealing?' The word caught her short.

'Clairmont the youth took a watch from the headmaster's study and hid it in his blankets. When it was found he admitted the theft and was sent down.'

Lillian felt her hands grip her side. Why was nothing ever easy as far as Lucas Clairmont was concerned? Why could she not find out something noble and virtuous about him instead of being plagued with a never-ending lack of moral fibre?

And why would a small boy steal a watch anyway? For money? To know the time? She could fathom neither the reason nor the risk. Why indeed had he not hidden it in a place no one would ever think to look? She took in a breath. No. She must not excuse him and take his side. Not for theft!

She was pleased when the older guests began to take their leave and was able to gladly follow, John accompanying her upstairs to her room.

'It has been a pleasure to be in your company today, Lillian,' he said as she opened her door, and she had the distinct impression that he was angling to kiss her again.

Consequently she sneezed three times, holding her handkerchief across her mouth and sniffing.

'My goodness, perhaps I have caught Aunt Jean's cold?'

'Will I call the housekeeper and ask her for some medicine?' The amorous look in his eyes was completely overtaken by concern.

'No, please do not bother. If I just go to sleep early…' She stopped and sneezed again and he moved back.

'Well, I suppose this is goodnight?' The words were said awkwardly and with disappointment.

'Thank you for walking me up.'

'It was my pleasure.'

She stepped inside and closed the door, standing still on the other side and replacing her handkerchief in her pocket. One night down and one more to go! Tomorrow she would make certain that she came up with the women in order to ensure no repeat performance of John's eagerness in seeing her alone.

Chapter Nine

A riding expedition seemed to be the entertainment for the next afternoon and as a keen horsewoman Lillian was looking forward to the freedom of racing across the Kentish countryside, though the eastern sky was draped in black billowing cloud.

Lucas Clairmont was again distant; he had tipped his hat as he had passed her, making his way to his horse, but he neither stopped in conversation nor offered to help her mount. John on the other hand was all attentive vigilance and her heart sank. Lucas Clairmont was due to return to America at the end of December, and would not return for many a long, long year, if ever. She was running out of time, the month of December almost upon them, and her father's demands of a Christmas engagement beginning to look more and more worrying.

Pulling her cloak around her neck to make the fur collar sit up, she ordered the horse on. A sorrel mare, it was neither fancy nor plain and its disposition as far as she could tell was pleasant. A horse much like the man who rode beside her, seeing to her every whim.

Caroline Shelby's mount trotted between St Auburn and Luc, her laughter returning on the eddy of wind to the rear of the pack. Three other couples completed the group, the Pagets conspicuous by their absence; Lillian presumed them to have packed their things and left. She sighed, hoping her father would not meet the odious man at his club and hear the story of her defence of Mr Clairmont as only he would probably see it. She seldom made enemies of people and the fact that she had worried her.

'Lady St Auburn has not joined us this morning.'

John's tone was puzzled.

'Perhaps she will later,' Lillian ventured, though she, too, had been surprised by Cassandra's absence. In fact, if she thought about it, she was also surprised by the closeness of the relationship between the St Auburns and Luc Clairmont. Nathaniel had said that he had been to see him in Virginia. Had Cassandra gone as well? Tonight she would make certain that she asked Cassie of the details and ask her also as to the size of any land Lucas Clairmont owned.

If only he were… what? she ventured. Rich? Well liked? Connected to the right people? Her musings took on a shallowness that she would have thought abhorrent in others. Yet she could not pursue a man whose very presence aroused such strong condemnation in those about him.

The strictures and codes that applied to everyday social life were after all there for a reason and the protection that they afforded was comforting. Even John's own layer of conventionality heartened her, for at least she could control him.

Luc Clairmont would be raw and ungovernable. The words made her wonder. He would not be repelled by a few false sneezes as John had been last night or distracted along any lines that she might favour. He would not be cajoled or dominated or managed. She remembered his kisses and her own unrestrained reaction to them and breathed in hard.

No. No. No.

Safety lay in correct behaviour, just as ruin lurked in the narrow margins of error and she would do very well to remember it. Sighing loudly, she tipped her head to the sky and decided that his entrancement with the Shelby heiress was probably for the best, though another feeling lingering beneath propriety wanted to scratch the woman's eyes out. Oh, she was beautiful, there was no doubt about that. But she was also more than forward, a girl who would eye up her quarry and go for it, and here her quarry was definitely Lucas Clairmont.

The clap of thunder came as they wound their way into a meadow almost at the edge of the St Auburn land, and everybody reined in their horses. Everyone, that is, except for Caroline Shelby, whose mount bolted towards a copse some few hundred yards away. Her screams this time were truly alarming, the timbre of them sending Lillian's own heels against the flank of her steed in pursuit.

Luc Clairmont, however, was in front of her already, his stallion galloping down upon the smaller mare and catching up with each long stride.

'Keep your head down,' he called to the terrified girl, 'and hold on.'

Caroline Shelby, however, seemed frozen solid, her gait unsteady and swaying. Another few yards and she would be off and if the stirrup wrapped about her boot was not freed she would also be dragged.

'Get your boots out of the stirrups,' Luc was now yelling. 'Or you will be unseated and caught.'

'I ca…aaa…aan't.' At least some advice seemed to be getting through even though she chose to ignore it, lying across her horse in a position that suggested pure and frozen terror.

Luc was at her side, leaning down wide from his own horse in a way that made Lillian's heart flutter. Goodness, if he were to fall in this position he would be under the hooves of both mounts and the jagged up-standing stones that scattered the field were not helping his cause either.

She shouted to him to be careful, sheer muscle and strength now keeping him in his seat, his centre of gravity so tilted as he tried unsuccessfully to rein in Lady Shelby's horse.

Freeing his feet from his stirrups as the edge of the copse bore down upon them, in a daring leap of faith he jumped from his horse to the other and grabbed on the reins, the bridle pulling at the horse's mouth and bringing its head back in a jerk.

The leafy green branches of the first oaks swiped him as he stopped, Caroline Shelby's crying now at a fever pitch as she clung to him, arms entwined about his neck as though she would never let him go.

Lillian drew her own horse up a second or so later and slid off.

'Are you hurt, Lady Shelby?' she asked anxiously, and caught the golden glance of Luc Clairmont.

'Not as badly as I am,' he drawled and extricated himself from the woman's grasp, jumping down from the horse. Touching a bloodied cheek he smiled, but after the fear of the last few moments any humour was lost on Lillian. She almost lifted her riding crop and hit him.

'Hurt? You could have been killed!' She made no attempt at all to curb her shout. 'You could have fallen and broken your head open on the stones or been trampled by the hooves of these frightened horses.'

Caroline Shelby's cornflower-blue eyes were now upon her, her terrified shrieks silenced. Gracious, Lillian thought, I have become exactly like her with such an outpouring of words. She clamped her mouth shut and turned away, bringing her whip down against a tree branch, liking the way the brown leaves fell at the action.

She was shaking, she felt it first in her hands and then in her stomach and as she took another step in the direction of her horse, a light-headed strangeness suddenly overcame her, a dry-mouthed fear that was overwhelming. Then the ground was swallowed by blackness and she could not stop her fall.

Luc caught her as she staggered the last few paces, her soft smallness easy to lift, her pale hair undone from its tight chignon as her hat fell to the ground. Her hair tumbled silver across his chest as he placed her gently on the grass.

'Lilly. Lilly.' He tapped her cheek and was rewarded by her eyes opening, shadow-bruised in uncertainty as she tried to sit up.

'Stay still. You fainted.'

'I…never…faint,' she returned, though a frown deepened as she realised that indeed she just had. 'It was your foolishness that made me…'

'I'm not hurt.'

Her thumb reached up to touch the blood on his cheek. He turned into the contact.

'From the branches,' he qualified, 'and just a scratch.'

Sweat marked her upper lip now and made her skin clammy. God, he could see Wilcox-Rice bearing down and he did not look happy. Behind him came the Hammonds. Nat was last and Luc could have sworn he had a smile on his face.

'I wanted to tell you that I felt something, too.' Her words were softly whispered, just before John claimed her and Lady Hammond bent to his side.

The kiss. She spoke of that? He knew she did. The

words on the card he had sent said the same thing. Caroline Shelby stood behind him now, looking at them strangely, gratitude mixed with shock. Had she heard? Would she say? He made much of picking his hat up and wiping it against his riding breeches.

'It seems the world is full of damsels in distress today,' he quipped and stepped away, hating to leave Lilly behind him with a fear of everything in her ashen face and pale eyes.

Everybody fussed over her, made her comfortable, tucked in her blankets and fluffed her pillows. Aunt Jean, Lady Hammond and Caroline Shelby. Even Cassandra St Auburn with her red hair floating about her face, and looking the picture of glowing good health. Why had she not joined her guests and could she get her alone for five minutes to ask the questions that she wanted to?

Lillian was glad in a way for this bed, glad to be sequestered in a room far away from the chance of meeting Lucas Clairmont again after her last whispered and most unwise remark.

'I wanted to tell you that I felt something, too.'

What had she been thinking? She shut her eyes against the horror of it all and Aunt Jean's voice was worried as she shook her arm.

'Are you feeling poorly again, my dear? Should I send for your father?' Her query was accompanied by a hacking cough that made Lillian draw the sheet further over her face for fear of catching it.

'No, I am perfectly all right, Aunt.' *And perfectly stupid,* she added beneath her breath.

Could she just stay hidden, pleading some illness that was inexplicable? But how then could she journey home? Gracious, if she had been in London this would have been a whole lot easier, but she was here at a country house an hour's drive away and in close proximity to a man to whom her reaction gave her a lot to be concerned over.

She could not trust herself, she decided, doom spreading at the conclusion.

She was now a feckless and insubstantial woman who did not trust her own mind and whose opinion was forever yo-yoing between this idea and that one.

To love him!

To love him not!

A man can smile and smile and be a villain!

Lucas had said so as he had spoken of his own shadows and mirrors and alluded that she might have her secrets too. Well, she did, and it was a secret that she could never tell anybody.

She…loved…him.

And she had done from the very first second of laying her eyes upon him outside the retiring room at the Lenningtons' ball. Loved a man with a smile in his eyes and a voice that held the promise of every single thing that she was not.

Brave. Free. Wild. Untethered.

And today with the chance of death dogging his

bravery she had recognised it, her very heart pierced with the impossibility.

'Oh, Lord God, help me, please…'

The prayer circled in her head, another petition to smite from her soul the horrible recognition of what was there.

Cassie St Auburn now sat on a chair near her bed, all the other women gone for the moment, and yet in her newly found revelation she did not dare to ask anything about Lucas Clairmont. What if he was a villain? What if he truly did inhabit the underworld of crime and gambling? What if she as a friend who knew him well warned her off?

'I am glad to see you better, Cassandra,' she began, at least filling the silence with something.

'Oh, I am only ever sick at mid-day. After that I am always much recovered.'

Lillian could not quite get the gist of her illness.

'I am pregnant,' Cassandra St Auburn laughed. 'Already halfway along.'

A great surge of envy overcame puzzlement. Cassie had a husband who loved her and was now awaiting her first child. With her smiles and happiness she had a life that Lillian suddenly felt was very far from her own. A solitary quiet life, her father's daughter, and burdened with a stalwart code of behaviour that was beginning to look faintly ludicrous and infinitely lonely.

'Lord Wilcox-Rice has been asking after you almost hourly,' Cassie continued, 'though I have made it clear to him that you need your rest.'

'Thank you.'

'Nat also had the doctor look at Mr Clairmont's injuries, but apart from a torn nail and a cut that has needed to be stitched across his cheek he is in fine form. He also asked after your health.'

'He did?' She tried to keep the interest from her question, but knew that she had not succeeded.

'Indeed. He felt somehow responsible for your faint.'

Lillian nodded and looked away. 'I thought that he might have been killed.'

'Nathaniel says that Lucas is a man who can easily look after himself.'

'I do not doubt it.'

'The wound on his cheek makes him look even more unruly than he normally does.'

'But it is not deemed dangerous to his health?' Lillian hated the tremor of worry in her words and hoped Cassie would not detect it.

'I doubt the doctor could have made Lucas stay in bed to rest even had the injury been worse.'

'I believe Mr Clairmont will be returning to America at the end of December? Has he already arranged passage?' Goodness, and she had promised herself that she would find out nothing, but Cassandra stood and looked at the time on a clock by the bedside table.

'I must not wear you out as the doctor asked for quiet and I think it might be wise for you to sleep.'

When she was gone Lillian wondered about her quick exit. Her hostess had not wished to answer any questions about Lucas Clairmont, that much she could glean. Why ever not? Were the St Auburns in on some sort of ruse? The headache she had been pretending for the past hour suddenly became real and she closed her eyes against the growing pain.

Caroline Shelby waylaid Luc in the drawing room after dinner and he wished he had left the salon when the other men had. She looked rather excited, her colour high and her eyes bright.

'I would like to thank you again for your help, Mr Clairmont.'

As she had already thanked him numerous times he held his counsel and waited.

'I would also like to ask you a question.' She looked around to make certain that there was no one behind her, eavesdropping. When she saw the coast was clear she continued, albeit a little more softly. 'I would like to ask you of the relationship between you and Lillian Davenport?'

'Miss Davenport?' A hammer swung against the beat of his heart. She had heard Lilly's words and everything was dangerous. Fury leaked into caution and into that came the obvious need for sense.

'I stopped her falling when she fainted. Something I would have done for any woman.'

'Any woman?' Lady Shelby looked relieved. 'So there are no special feelings between you?'

'There are not. I barely know her.'

'Then would I be remiss to ask you if you might accompany me home on the morrow? I need to be back in London and would appreciate an escort.'

'Of course,' Luc answered. 'I would be delighted.'

When she had left he poured himself a large cold drink of water.

Nat found him forty minutes later sitting watching the night through the opened curtains.

'You are not in bed?'

'I am leaving with Caroline Shelby first thing in the morning.'

'A change of plans, then?'

'The woman came right out and implied I had feelings for Lilly Davenport.'

'Lilly?'

'And I haven't.'

'Of course not.'

'I would ruin her.'

'Lord, Luc. Sometimes I think that you are too hard on yourself and Virginia is far from here.'

'It is my home, the only one I have known.'

'Only because you refused to ever come back.'

'No.' Anger was infused in the word. Real anger. 'You do not understand…'

'And God only knows how I wish I could, but you will not let me in! There is something you are not telling me, and if there is one person in the world who owes you a favour you are looking right at him. After Eton…'

'None of it was your fault, Nat.'

'It was me who stole the watch, remember, and you

who took the blame.' This confession was said with such a sense of doom that Luc began to laugh.

'Lord, Nathaniel, it was your damn watch in the first place and the master had no right in taking it.'

'Still, it was not one of my finest moments and I always regretted such a lapse in courage.'

'You just wanted your property back and I was desperate to be gone. Each of us gained what we hoped for. You know that.'

'If you had stayed in England, I could have helped you.'

'Getting expelled from Eton saved me, because with my mother and father out of the country, I had a chance to escape them and become my own man.'

'You were fourteen.'

'Going on twenty.' Luc took another sip of the water in his glass. 'And you and Hawk were the only damn friends that I ever had there.'

'Not much of a friend, I fear. Look at Paget bringing up the past like it was yesterday.'

'He is a man who still has much of the boy in him.'

'And there is the trouble of it all, Luc. People here are long on memory and short on forgiveness and without a family name to shelter behind you are open game. If we came back to town and you moved in with us…'

'I think it wiser to keep a distance, Nat.'

'Because of your intelligence work? You said it was over and finished. You said that you no longer worked for the army in any capacity.'

'I don't, but there are remnants of other things that don't so easily fade.'

The moon suddenly came out from behind the clouds and through the open curtains the landscape around this tiny corner of Kent was bathed in light. Touching the newly stitched scar on his cheek, Luc stood and downed the last of his drink. 'You're a family man now, Nat, with the promise of a child come the summer. Concentrate on those things, aye.'

On the silver lawn an owl swooped, its talons catching a field mouse in full flight, taking it up into the sky, a small and struggling prey that had been in the wrong place at the wrong time.

Like himself as a youngster, Luc thought, and unlatched the ties so that the curtains fell across the scene in a single heavy tumble of burgundy velvet.

Chapter Ten

'There is some evil afoot, Lillian,' her father said quietly as she lifted the first of the Christmas garlands into place around the hearth in the blue salon. 'Lord Paget has been found dead at his house this morning.'

Lillian fastened the bough of pine before turning, trying to give herself some sense of time.

'But he was with us at the weekend at the St Auburns.'

'Which brings me to the very reason that I mention it. Some are saying that his death is suspicious for there was an argument, it seems, between him and Clairmont. The American has been taken in for questioning.'

'But Mr Clairmont did not cause the argument, Father, he tried to stop it.'

'Oh, well, no doubt the constabulary will get to the bottom of what happened and it's hardly our problem. From all accounts the man is a renegade and why he continues to frequent the soirées of the *ton* eludes me.

I for one would not give him the time of day.' Standing beside her, he put his hand up to the greenery. 'That looks lovely—will you place one on the other side too?'

Lillian nodded, though the Christmas spirit had quite gone out of her as she thought back to the weekend.

Luc Clairmont had already left when she had finally risen on the Sunday morning, accompanying Lady Caroline Shelby back to London! He had not stayed to find out more about her hastily whispered promise of feeling 'something' and had not tried to contact her since.

Could he have murdered the man? For an insult? Her whole world was turning upside down and she had no way of stopping it doing so.

The pile of decorations she had had the maid bring down from the attic lay before her, a job she usually enjoyed, but now… She looked over at the tin soldiers and varnished collages, the paper cornucopias all waiting to be filled and the hand-dipped candles that she had so lovingly fashioned last year. A pile of gay Christmas cards lay further afield and the dolls she used every Yuletide in the nativity scene beneath the tree were neatly packed in another box. All waiting!

When a maid came to say that there was a caller and gave her the card of Caroline Shelby, she was almost relieved to be able to put off the effort of it all.

'Please show her up,' she instructed the girl and Lady Shelby appeared less than a scant moment later.

'Miss Davenport! I am so sorry to intrude, but I have come on a matter of a most delicate sort.'

Gesturing for the newcomer to sit, Lillian took the chair opposite and waited for her to begin. 'It's just I do not know what to do and you are so sensible and seem to know just exactly what next step to take about everything.'

Lillian smiled through surprise and felt a lot older than the young and emotional girl opposite.

'The thing is that I have found myself becoming increasingly attracted to Mr Lucas Clairmont from Virginia and I came because I heard you talking to him when you were recovering after your faint.'

'I beg your pardon?' Of everything Caroline Shelby might have said this was the most unforeseen, and she hoped her own rush of emotion was not staining her face.

'At the St Auburns'. I heard you say that you felt something for him.'

Lillian made herself smile, the danger in the girl's announcement very alarming. 'Perhaps you have made an error, Lady Shelby, for I am about to be engaged to Lord Wilcox-Rice.'

The woman looked uncertain. 'I had not heard that.'

'Probably because you were too busy fabricating untruths,' she returned. 'John and I have been promised to each other for the past three weeks and my father has given us his blessing.'

Caroline Shelby stood, placing her bag across the crook of her arm. 'Oh, well then, I shall say no more about any of it and ask most sincerely for your pardon of my conduct. I would also ask you, in the light of all that has been revealed, to keep the words spoken between us private. I should not wish any others to know.'

'Of course not.'

She rang the bell and the maid came immediately.

'I bid you good afternoon, Lady Shelby.' Lillian could hear the coldness in her words.

'Good afternoon, Miss Davenport.'

Once the woman had gone she sat down heavily on the couch. Gracious, could this day become any worse? She did not think that it possibly could although she was mistaken.

Half an hour later John Wilcox-Rice arrived beaming.

'I have just seen Lady Shelby and she led me to believe that you had had second thoughts about our engagement.'

Lillian looked at him honestly for the first time in weeks. He was an ordinary man, some might even say a boring man, but he was not a murderer or a liar. Today his eyes were bright with hope and in his hands he held a copy of a book she had mentioned she would like to read whilst staying at the St Auburns'. She added 'a thoughtful man' to her list.

'Perhaps we should speak to Father.'

Ernest Davenport broke open his very best bottle of champagne and poured four glasses, her aunt Jean being summoned from her rooms to partake in the joyous news.

'I cannot tell you how delighted I am with this announcement, Lillian. John here will make you a fine husband and your property will be well managed.'

Her aunt Jean, not wishing to be outdone in gladness, clapped her hands. 'When did you think to have the wedding, Lillian?'

'We can decide on a date after Christmas, Aunt,' she replied, the whole rigmarole of organising the occasion something she did not really wish to consider right now.

'And a dress, we must find the most beautiful gown, my dear. Perhaps a trip to Paris to find it might be in order, Ernest?'

Her father laughed, a sound Lillian had not heard in many months and her anxiety settled. 'That seems like a very good idea to me, Jean.'

John had come to stand near her, and he took her fingers in his own.

'You have made me the happiest of fellows, my dear Lillian, the very happiest.'

My dear? Goodness, he sounded exactly like her father. What would she call him? No name at all came to mind as she went over to the drinks table and helped herself to another generous glass of champagne, turning only when Eleanor was shown in by the maid, a look of surprise on her face.

'I have just been given the news,' she said, 'and so I have come immediately. Mama and Papa are returning from the country tonight so the timing could not have been better.'

With a smile she enveloped Lillian in her arms. 'And

you, sister-in-law—' the words rolled off her tongue in an impish way '—I didn't have an idea that you two were so close and you let me know nothing! Was it the sprig of mistletoe that settled it? When shall the ceremony take place? Do you already have your bridesmaids?'

Everyone laughed at the run of questions, except Lillian, who suddenly and dreadfully saw exactly what she had done. Not just she now and John, but her family and Eleanor and a group of people whom she did not wish in any way to hurt.

Taking a breath, she firmly told herself to stop this introspection and, finishing the champagne, bent to the task of answering the many questions Ellie was pounding her with.

A sensible and prudent husband...

The five words were like a mantra in the aching centre of her heart.

They had finally gone. All of them. Her father to his club and her aunt to a bridge party at an old friend's house. Eleanor and John had returned home to see if their parents had arrived from the country.

Four days ago she had fancied herself in love with one man and today she was as good as married to another. The very notion of it made her giggle. Was this what they termed a hysterical reaction? she wondered when she found it very hard to stop. Tears followed, copious and noisy and she was glad for the sturdy lock on the door and the lateness of the hour.

Carefully she stood and walked to the book on the shelf in which she had pressed one orange bloom. The flower was almost like paper now, a dried-up version of what it once had been. Like her? She shook her head. All of this was not her fault, for goodness' sake! She had made a choice based on facts, a choice that any woman of sound mind might have also made.

The Davenport property was a legacy, after all, one that needed to be minded by each generation for the next one. The man she would marry had to be above question, reputable and unflinchingly honest. He could not be someone who was considered a suspect in a murder case. Besides, Luc Clairmont had neither called on her in town since she had made her ridiculous confession nor tried in any way to show he reciprocated her feelings.

Her fingers tightened on the flower. She was no longer young and the proposals of marriage, once numerous, had trickled away over the past year or two.

Caroline Shelby's exuberant youth was the embodiment of a new wave of girls, a group who had begun to make their own rules in the way they lived their lives.

Poor Lillian.

The conversation from the retiring room over three weeks' ago returned in force.

Everything had changed in the time between then and now! A tear traced its way down her cheek, and she swiped it away. No, she would not cry. She had made the right and only choice, and if John Wilcox-Rice's kisses did not set her heart to beating in the same way as Luc Clairmont's did, then more fool she. Marriage was about much more than just lust, it was about respect and honour and regard and surely as the years went by these things would gain in ascendancy.

Feeling better, she placed the flower back in the book and tucked it on to the shelf. A small memento, she thought, of a time when she had almost made a silly mistake. She wondered why her hands felt so empty when the orange bloom was no longer in them.

His father's face was above him red with anger, the strap in his hands biting into thin bare legs. Further off his mother sat, head bent over her tapestry and not looking up.

Screaming when silence was no longer possible, William Clairmont's beating finally ceased, though the agony of his parents' betrayal was more cutting than any slice of leather.

'Another lesson learnt, my boy,' his father said, trailing his fingers softly down the side of his son's face. 'We will say no more of this, no more of any of it. Understood?'

Luc woke up sweating, trying to fight his way out of the blankets, cursing both the darkness and the ghost of his father. If he had been here now, even in a celestial form, he would have made a fist and beaten him out of hiding, the love that most normal fathers felt for their children completely missing in his.

As fury dimmed, the room took shape and the sounds of the early morning formed, shadows passing into the promise of daylight. He hadn't had this particular dream for years and he wondered what had brought it on. Nat's mention, he supposed, of the Eton fiasco, and the events that had followed.

The knock on the door made him freeze.

'Everything in order, Luc?' Stephen Hawkhurst's head came around the portal, the fact that he was still in his evening clothes at this time of the morning raising Luc's eyebrows.

'You've been out all night?' The smell of fine perfume wafted in with him.

'You refused to join me, remember? Nat had an excuse in the warm arms of his wife, but you?' He came in to the small room and lay across the bottom of the bed, looking up. 'Elizabeth has been dead for months and if you don't let the guilt go soon you never will.'

'Nathaniel's already given me the same lecture, thanks, Hawk.' Luc didn't like the coldness he could hear in his own words.

'And as you have not listened to either of us I have another solution. Leave this place and move in with me and I'll throw the grandest ball of the Season and make certain that anyone who is anyone is there. Properly done it could bury the whispers of your past for ever, and as the guest of honour with Nat and me beside you, who would dare to question?' A smile began to form on Stephen's face. 'You're a friend of Miss Davenport's. If we can get her and her fiancé to come, then all the others will follow.'

'She is engaged to Wilcox-Rice!' Luc tried to keep his alarm hidden.

'I heard it said this evening and on good authority that the wedding will be after Christmas…'

'The devil take it!' Luc's curse stopped Hawkhurst in his tracks.

'What did I miss?'

'Nothing, Hawk,' Luc replied, 'you missed nothing at all, and I should have damned well known better.'

A whoop of delight made his heart sink. 'You are enamoured by Miss Davenport? The saint and the sinner, the faultless and the blemished, the guilty and the guiltless. Lord, I could go on all night.' Hawk was in his element now, fingers drumming against the surface of the blankets as he mulled over his options. Luc sat up against the headboard and wished to hell that he had said nothing.

'I suppose you could always hope that Wilcox-Rice will bore her to death?'

'I could.' From past experience Luc knew it was better to humour him.

'But with the wedding planned for early next year that probably won't give you enough time.'

'That soon?'

'Apparently. Davenport is her cousin, you know that, don't you, so when you wrap your arm around his neck next time, best to do it out of sight of your lady.'

'She isn't my lady.'

'An attitude like that won't effect any change.'

'Enough, Stephen. It's early and I am tired.'

His friend frowned. 'Nat and I were the closest to brothers you ever had, Luc, so if you want to talk about anything…'

'I don't.'

'But you would not be adverse to the ball?'

'You were always the problem solver.'

'Oh, and another thing. When I was out tonight I heard from a source that the police have determined Paget's death as suicide and we both know what that means.'

'I won't be had up for his murder!'

'If you stopped harassing Davenport and quit the gambling tables, you wouldn't be a suspect and, to my mind, Daniel Davenport isn't worth the trouble no matter what he has done to make you believe otherwise.'

'My wife might have disagreed.'

'Elizabeth knew him?' Surprise coated the query.

'If the letter Davenport sent her was any indication of the feelings between them, she knew him very well.'

'Hell.' Luc liked the shock in Hawk's word, for he had begun to question his own reactions to all that he was doing.

'If you kill him, you'll hang. Better to do away with him on some dark night far from London'

'Shift the blame, you mean?' He laughed as Hawk nodded and felt the best he had done in months.

'On reflection I don't think it was all her fault. Towards the end I liked her as little as she did me.' Honesty was a double-edged sword and Luc wished he could have had Hawk's black-and-white view of the picture.

'When did you become so equitable?'

Unexpectedly Lillian's face came to Luc's mind. She had tempered his anger and loneliness and despair and replaced his feeling of dislocation with a trust and belief in goodness that was…staggering and warming all at the same time.

'It's age, I think.' He smiled as he said it and knew that his words were a complete lie. As the first birdsong lilted into the new morning Stephen stretched and yawned.

'I have to go to sleep. Goodnight, Luc.'

'Goodnight, Hawk.'

When his oldest friend simply curled up at the bottom of his bed and was soon snoring, Lucas smiled. There were definitely advantages to being back in England and Stephen was one of them.

The following morning he left Stephen still asleep in his lodgings and walked along the Thames, the winter whipping the river into grey waves that swelled up the embankment and threatened to engulf the pathway. He didn't want to go to a club or a tavern or even to the Lindsay town house where he always felt welcome. No, today he simply walked, on past the Chelsea Hospital and down the route that the body of Wellington must had been taken during his state funeral last November. A million people had lined the streets then, it was said, and they would again at the next funeral, the next celebration, the next public function that caught the fancy of a nation.

Life went on despite a wife who had betrayed him and an uncle who had died well before his time.

Stuart Clairmont!

Even now the name was hard to say and he ground his teeth together to try to stop the sorrow that welled up over the thought. A man who had been the father his own never was. A man who had loved and nurtured a lost child newly come from England and given him back the sense of purpose and strength that had been leached away from him under the punitive regime of a father who thought punishment to be the making of character.

He still bore the scars of such bestial brutality and still hated William Clairmont with all the passion of a young boy who had never stood a chance.

Where was Lilly? he wondered, the news of her engagement angering him again. She would marry a man who was patently wrong for her, a man who neither kissed her with any skill nor fought with a scrap of dexterity. He remembered the feeble slap Wilcox-Rice had given Paget before he had intervened, the breathless sheen on his face from the effort of doing even that, pointing to a spouse who would not protect a wife from anyone.

The flaws in his argument pressed in. John Wilcox-Rice was a man who would not have enemies, his life lived in the narrow confines of an untarnished society. Why should he need to be adept at the darker arts of survival, the things that kept a man apart and guarded? As he was!

The number of differences between Lillian and him spiralled upwards as he ran for the omnibus, and as the conductor inside issued him a ticket for the cramped and smelly space he was certain that the permitted twenty-two passengers was almost twice that number.

Chapter Eleven

No one was speaking to Lucas Clairmont, Lillian saw as she walked into the Billinghurst soirée that evening and found it was divided into two distinct camps.

Oh, granted, the Earl of St Auburn and Lord Hawkhurst leaned against the columns on his side of the room, the smiles on their faces looking remarkably genuine, but nobody else went near him.

It was the death of Lord Paget, she supposed, and the fact that much was said about the card games Lucas Clairmont was involved with. Gossip that did not quite accuse him of cheating, but not falling much short either.

'Mr Clairmont does seem to inspire strong feelings in people, doesn't he?'

Lillian looked around quickly, trying to determine if her friend was including herself in that category.

Lucas Clairmont looked vividly handsome on the

other side of the room, dressed in a formal black evening suit that he looked less than comfortable in.

'If he is here and not languishing in a London gaol, my guess would be the police thought him to have no knowledge of Lord Paget's death.'

Anne Weatherby at her side laughed at the summation. 'You are becoming quite the defender of the man, Lillian. I heard it was your testimony at the St Auburns that had the Pagets fleeing in the first place.'

'And for that I now feel guilty.'

'Well, your husband-to-be seems to have no such thoughts. He looks positively radiant this evening.'

John crossed the room towards them, Eleanor on his arm, and indeed he did look very pleased with himself.

'I have it on good authority that Golden Boy is set to run a cracking first at Epsom this year and as he is a steed I have a financial stake in the news is more than pleasing. Is your father here, Lillian? I must go and impart the news to him.'

Eleanor watched as her brother chased off again across the room and entwined her arm through Lillian's.

'I do believe that John loves your father almost as much as he loves you. He is always telling me that Ernest Davenport says this and Ernest Davenport says that. My own papa must be getting increasingly tired of having the endless comparisons, I fear, though in all honesty John hasn't seen eye to eye with him for a very long time. The inherent competition, I suspect, between generations so closely bound. I often wonder if a spell in India or in the army might have finished my brother off well? Pity, perhaps, that that avenue is no longer available.'

Lillian tried to imagine John in the wilds of the Far East and found that she just could not. He was a man who seemed more suited to the ease of the drawing room.

Lucas Clairmont on the other hand never looked comfortable confined in the small spaces of London society. Oh, granted, he had a sort of languid unconcern written across him here as he conversed with his friends, but he never relaxed, a sense of animated vitality not quite extinguished. He also always stood with his back against the wall, a trait that gave the impression of constant guardedness. The guise of a soldier, perhaps, or something darker. She had read the stories of Colquhoun Grant and there was something in the character of Wellington's head of intelligence that was familiar in the personality of the man who stood opposite her.

As if he sensed her looking at him, his eyes turned to meet her own, dark gold glinting with humour. Quickly she looked away and made much of adjusting the pin on her bodice. When she glanced back, he no longer watched her and she squashed the ridiculous feeling of disappointment.

Turning the ring John had given her on her betrothal finger, she tried to take courage from it as she listened to the conversation between Anne and Eleanor.

'I hear that congratulations are in order,' he said in a quiet tone as they met an hour later by one of the pillars in a largely deserted supper room. 'Your groom-to-be must have made great strides in the art of kissing a woman.'

'Indeed, Mr Clairmont,' Lillian replied, 'and although you may not credit it, there are, in truth, other things that are of much more importance.'

'There are?' His surprise made it difficult to maintain her sense of decorum.

'A man's reputation for one,' she bit back, 'is considered by a careful bride to be essential.'

'And are you a careful bride, Lilly?'

'Lillian,' she echoed, ignoring the true intent of his question. 'And careful in the way of being certain that John has at least never been a suspect in murder.'

'Because he plays everything as safely as you do?'

She turned, but he caught at her arm, not gently either, the hard bite of his fingers making her flinch. 'Perhaps you might wait till the findings of the police are made public before naming me guilty.'

'Why?' she retaliated. 'If you keep the company of gamblers and card sharps and are often covered in the bruises and markings of a man who goes from one squabble to the next, why indeed should I give you any leeway?'

'Because I hope you know by now, Lilly, that I am not quite as black as you would paint me.' His accent was soft but distinct, the cadence of the new lands on his tongue.

'Do I, Lucas? Do I know that?'

It was the first time she had called him by his Christian name and the warm glow in his eyes alarmed her. There was something else there too. A vulnerability that she had not seen before, an unprotected and exposed need that tugged at her because it was so unexpected.

'Marrying one man because of the faults of another is not the wisest of choices.'

'So what is it then you would suggest?'

He laughed, the sound filling the empty space around them. 'Come away with me instead.'

The room whirled, a yearning ache in her body that she was completely astonished by. If only he meant it. If only the laughter that the invitation had been accompanied with did not sound quite so offhand. So casual!

'And spend the rest of my life wondering when a noose would be placed about your neck?'

'I had nothing to do with the death of Paget, if that is what you are implying.'

'You were asked to leave Eton.'

'I was a boy…'

'Who stole a watch?'

Again he began to laugh. 'Such a crime…' But she allowed his amusement no further rein.

'I am the only heir to Fairley Manor, Mr Clairmont, and in England we protect our assets by marrying wisely.'

He tipped his head and in the light of the room Lillian saw the beginnings of a reddened scar that snaked from his right ear into the collar of his shirt.

'A long-ago accident,' he qualified as he saw her uncertainty.

But she was transfixed. This was no simple wound that would take a day or two to mend. She imagined both the pain and the tenacity needed to recover from such an injury and in her conjecture also saw the wide and yawning gap that lay between them. Who had tended him in his hours of need, wiped his brow and brought him water? She had heard it said he had left for America as a boy, but there had been no mention of any family.

'Did your parents go with you to the Americas?'

He looked puzzled at her change of topic. 'My parents?'

'The Earl of St Auburn implied that you were barely above fourteen when you left Eton and that you sailed from England very soon afterwards.'

'I had an uncle there already.'

'So you took passage alone?'

'Worked my way there actually as a deckhand on the *Joanna*. Forty days was all it took between London and New York—the seas and winds were kind.'

Marvelling at his description, she imagined a child making his way across the world to a different shore, the mantle of being labelled a thief on his shoulders and alone. Why had his parents not gone with him? She sensed he wanted no more questions as he stood there, the candles above setting his hair to a shade of lighter brown amongst the ebony, curling long against his nape.

'Wilcox-Rice will never make you happy.' The words seemed dragged from him.

'Whereas you will?'

He smiled at that. 'There are things more important than a certain cut of cloth or which fork one uses at a banquet table, Miss Davonport.'

'You think that is what defines me?'

'Partly.'

She hated the truth in his words and the answering echo of it in her own mind. 'The sum of my pieces must be awfully galling to you then, Mr Clairmont, just as the sum of your own is as equally trying to me. I think a passably good kiss in a man who seems to eschew every other moral principle would not sustain a relationship for even as long as a month.'

'Do you now?' Ground out. Barely civil.

Lillian stood her ground. 'Indeed, for it has come to my ears that the whisper of friendship and respect is a most underrated thing in any marriage.'

'Which unfulfilled brides have told you that nonsense?'

Shock held her rigid. 'Perhaps it was naïve of me to expect that you might consider such a sentiment with an open mind.'

'An open mind?' He laughed. 'When your own has just condemned me as a murderer.'

'Paget was a man you seemed to have much reason to hate.'

'I concede. Put like that my case seems hopeless and if a thought is as lethal as a bullet…'

When she allowed a smile to blossom he took the small chance of it quickly.

'Stay the night with me, Lillian. See what it is you will miss if you marry John Wilcox-Rice.'

The shock of his question was only overrun by the stinging want in her body. 'I could start with ruination—'

He broke into her banter. 'I would never hurt you, at least believe that.'

She saw the way he looked about to make certain no person lay in earshot, saw the way too he kept his hands jammed in his jacket pockets and his face carefully bland. They could for all intents and purposes be discussing the weather should a bystander take the time to watch them.

'If by some misguided logic I should chance to consider such a risky venture, where would you imagine this tryst to take place? I should not wish to shed my inhibitions in a dosshouse, after all.'

'Someone has told you my address?'

The dimple in his cheek was deep and she tried not to let the beauty of his face daunt her.

'Come away with me, then. I have a house in Bedfordshire.'

'I could not possibly…'

'You could buy a kiss when you barely knew me. Take that one step further.'

John Wilcox-Rice's voice sounded behind her. 'Lillian, I have been looking for you.' His words were wary and distrustful.

'Mr Clairmont has just extended an invitation to us

to call in at his house in the country.' She watched as amber flared, catching her glance in a hooded warning.

'I doubt we shall be in the district, Clairmont, and I thought I had heard it said that you were taking passage home very soon.'

'Unless the police have need to keep me in London.'

John stuttered at such nonchalance. A challenge. A provocation. A carefully worded gauntlet thrown into the ring between adversaries and John with no notion at all as to what he fought for.

Her!

The beat of Lillian's heart thickened in the dawning realisation that she was the prize, a situation that she had not had the experience of since her first year of coming out, and the band of white gold and diamonds on the third finger of her left hand felt tight, a small message of control and limit that constricted everything.

Oh, for the chance of another kiss? No, there wasn't the possibility for any of it, especially here with her father and aunt close and a fiancé who allowed her not a moment's respite. If only she might lay her fingers in those of the American opposite and simply walk, now, away from it all.

Like her mother had!

She shook her head and the moment of madness passed, evaporated into expectation and duty. Lillian or Lilly. The white and careful promise of obligation and discretion counterbalanced against the wilder orange flair of excitement and thrill.

The very same choices Rebecca had mismanaged all those years before and look where it had taken her: a deathbed racked with self-reproach and contrition.

She inclined her head as she allowed John Wilcox-Rice to take her arm and lead her out into the ballroom proper, the music of Strauss settling her fears as it swirled and eddied about them. Many in the pressing crowd smiled at them, the illusion of a wondrous young love, not such a difficult one to pass off after all.

John leaned in as they performed the waltz, the ardour that had been apparent at the St Auburns' the night he had escorted her to her room as obvious here.

She felt his fingers splayed out across her back.

'This is the dance of lovers, Lillian. Appropriate, don't you think?'

It took all of her composure not to break his hold and pull away.

'If you could give some consideration about naming a date for our nuptials, and preferably one in the not-too-distant future, you would make me the happiest of men.'

Lillian faltered. 'With all the Christmas preparations I have been busy.'

'What of February, then?'

'I had thought of the summer,' she returned and his face fell.

'No, that is too long.' The forceful tone in his voice surprised her. 'It needs to be earlier.'

Nodding, she retreated into silence. Earlier? The very word was like a death knell in her heart.

* * *

'If you don't approach her soon the night will be gone, Luc.' Hawkhurst's voice was insistent. Already the clock was nearing the hour of two.

'I think I made myself more than clear to Miss Davenport an hour or so back, Hawk.'

'And she wanted none of you?'

'Exactly.'

'Well, that's a first. So you're going to give up just like that?'

'I am. She intimated that she thought I had some hand in the death of Paget.'

'You are here for a month and life becomes interesting again. To my mind, however, Lillian Davenport seems downright miserable and the stuffed shirt of a fiancé looks as though he is hanging on to her arm for dear life. Even her father looks bored with his conversation and that's saying something.' He stopped, and Luc didn't like the way he smiled. 'Her aunt on the other hand is eyeing you up with a singular interest.'

'She probably wants to chastise me on behalf of her son.'

'No, the glance is one more of a measured curiosity.'

'Then perhaps she was a particular friend of Albert Paget and is trying to work out how I did away with him.'

'Well, no doubt we will discover the truth in a moment. She seems to be heading this way.'

'Alone?'

'Very.'

'Mr Clairmont.' Jean Taylor-Reid's voice carried across the room around them and, ignoring Hawkhurst altogether, she went straight to the heart of what was worrying her. 'I think my niece seems to have taken up your cause as a man who needs improvement and so I have come to warn you. There are many here who say that the misdemeanours of your youth would make it difficult for you to fashion a future here in London.'

'Is that what they say, Lady Taylor-Reid?' He looked around pointedly. 'England has long since ceased to frighten me with its obsession with the importance of family name and fortune.'

'Then you are inviting problems for yourself.'

'I beg your pardon?'

Ignoring his perplexity, she carried on. 'The protection offered by a family name is irrefutable and the name of Davenport is one I should wish to keep untainted. If my son Daniel has done anything to offend you…' She swallowed back tears and stopped, and Luc, who could not for the life of him work out where she was going with this, remained silent.

'I would plead with you to ignore him. He may not be the easiest person to like, but if he should die…' Her voice petered out, but, taking a breath, she continued more strongly. 'I would, of course, offer you something in return. There are whispers, you see, that you are more involved in the Paget death than you let on. Perhaps this might be a wise time to simply return to America—slip out on the next tide, so to speak. There is a ship leaving for Boston in the morning that has a berth which is paid for.' She pressed a paper into his hands. 'You will find all the details here, Mr Clairmont, and the captain is amenable to asking no questions.'

'Leaving both your son and niece safe from my person?'

'I think we understand each other entirely.'

She did not wait to see if he agreed, but moved away, back to the side of Lillian's father who watched with open anger. A small greying woman with a slight stoop and the iron will of a doyenne who would do anything to protect the reputation of her family.

'Perhaps Davenport learned the art of getting his own way in everything from the unlikely breast of his mother.'

Luc laughed at Stephen's reflection, though Lilly pointedly looked away from him, the tip-tilt of her nose outlined against the wall behind.

Beautiful. And careful. A woman whose life was lived and measured by the right thing to do. He should take note of Jean Taylor-Reid's warning, should leave Lillian Davenport to the faultless standards of an exacting *ton* and to a fiancé who would for ever be circumspect and judicious. But he could not, not when she had whispered her feelings to him after she had fainted and her guard was down, not when she had admitted that her favourite colour was orange when it was so plainly not.

He finished his glass of lemonade and placed the container on a low-lying table beside him. If he did not act tonight, tomorrow might be too late, the aunt's pro-

clivity to interference worrying and his own problems
with Davenport throwing him into a no-man's land of
wait and see.

He had never let anyone close, his wife's death a part
of that equation in a way he had not understood before.
Lillian was drawing something out of him that he
thought was gone, shrivelled up in the miserable years
of both his youth and his marriage. But it had not.
Tonight as he watched her across the room in her white
dress and with the candlelight in her hair, the hard
centre of his heart had begun to thaw, begun to hope,
begun again to feel the possibility of a life that was…
whole.

Swearing to himself, he turned away from Hawk and
strode out on to a balcony near the top of the room.

The strains of Mozart rent the air, soft, civilised, a
thread of memory from an England that had never quite
left him. A great well of yearning made him swallow.
Yearning for a home. Yearning for Lilly and her goodness, and sense and trust and honesty.

In the window of a salon downstairs he could see a
Christmas tree glowing, the candles on its bough
promising all that was right and good with the world.
Elizabeth had never fussed with such traditions, preferring instead an endless round of visiting. A woman who
found solace in the busy whirl of society.

He ran his hand through his hair. If he was honest he
had married her for her looks, a shallow reason that he
had had much cause to regret within the first year of

their life together. But he had been nearly twenty-seven and the land he had spent breaking in with Stuart had taken much of his time since first arriving in America. When she had come after him with her flashing eyes and chestnut curls he had been entranced.

He had never loved her! The thought made him swear because even in his darkest hours he had not admitted it to himself. Why now, though? Why here? He knew the answer even as he phrased the question. Because in the room beside this one a woman whom he felt more respect for than any other he had met in his life laughed and danced and chatted.

'I think my niece seems to have taken up your cause as a man who needs improvement and so I have come to warn you.'

The old woman's voice rang true in his conscience as he opened the door and searched the space inside, and as luck might have it Lilly separated herself from her family group and retired to a small alcove at one end of the room. Had she seen him coming? Lucas did not know. All he knew was that he was beside her in the quiet dimmed space and that her warmth beat at his coldness, living flame in her pale blue eyes. He could no longer be circumspect.

'Your aunt has just warned me away from you. She thinks I may be a corrupting influence.'

'And are you, Lucas? Are you that?'

He shook his head, her very question biting at certainty. He wanted to say more, but found himself stymied; after all, there had been much he had done in his life that she would not like. As if she could read his mind she faced him directly.

'I do not understand what this thing is between us, but how I wish that it would just stop.' She laid her hand across her chest as if her heartbeat was worrying her, and the sensation building inside him wound tighter, dangerously complete. There was no room left for compromise or bargain.

'I want you.' Sense and logic deserted him as his thumb traced a line down the side of her arm, the silver of her hair falling like mist across the blackness of his clothes.

Fragile. Easily ruined.

Even that thought did not have him pulling away, not tonight with this small chance of possibility all that was left to him. Now. Here. Only this minute lost in the luck of a provident encounter and a hundred-and-one reasons why he should just let her go. Her fingers joined his thumb and he chided himself, the thin daintiness of white silk sleeves falling over his fist like a shroud. Hidden.

'Lord.' He pulled back as he closed his eyes and swore, a softer feeling tugging at lust and settling wildness.

'Lilly.' Her name. Just that. He could not even whisper what it was he desired because even the saying of it would take away the beauty of imagination and, if memory was all he was to be left with, he would not spoil even a second of it by a careless entreaty.

* * *

He had both power and restraint. The disparity suited him, she thought, as the heat inside her crumbled any true resistance and the incomprehensible fragment of time between separation and togetherness ended. Like a dream, close as breath. Melding simply by touch into one being. She heard the echo of his heartbeat, fast and strong, felt the tremble of his fingers as they trailed down silk and met flesh beneath the lace at her elbows. Her own breath shallowed, roughly taken, the very start of something she could no longer fight, no words to deny him. Anything. She had had enough of denial and of pretending that everything she felt for him was a ruse.

Tears welled as she swallowed. 'If you kiss me here, I shall be ruined.'

There was no choice left though, for already her body leaned across, breasts grazing his shirt beneath an opened jacket, nipples hardened with pure and simple desire. He was her only point of connection in the room, her north to his south, balanced and equal. Even facing havoc she wanted him, wanted him to touch her, to kiss her as he had before and show her what it was that could exist between a man and a woman when everything was exactly as it should be.

Before it was all too late. She did not dare to fight it any longer for fear of a loss that would be more than she could bear! A single tear dropped on to her cheek and she felt its passage like a hot iron, wrenching right from wrong, and changing before to after. No will of her own left. Just what would be between them, here in this room, fifteen feet from her father and fiancé and from three hundred prying eyes.

'Ah, Lilly, if only this were the way of it.' His voice was sad with a hint of resignation in the message as he lifted her hand and kissed the back of it. She felt his tongue lave between the base of her fingers, warm and wet with promise. When he moved back she tried to hold him, tried to catch on to what she knew was lost already. But he did not stay, did not turn as he left the alcove, light swallowing up both shadow and boldness.

Gone.

Alone she trembled, her fists clenched before her, the words of a childhood prayer murmured in a bid for composure, and her nails biting into the heated flesh of her palms.

Life is like a river and it takes you where you are meant to be.

Here. Without him!

She looked out into the night, a myriad of stars above shifting bands of lower cloud. The weather had changed just as she had. She could feel it in her blood and in the rising welling joy that recognised honour.

Lucas Clairmont's honour just to leave her, safe. Taking a deep breath for confidence, she turned and almost bumped into the Parker sisters, cold horror on their faces. The beat of her heart rose so markedly that she felt her throat catch in fear. Coughing, she tried to find speech. Had they seen? Could they know?

'It is a lovely evening.' Even to her ears the words sounded forced, the tremble in them pointing at all that she tried so hard to hide.

But they did not answer back, did not smile or speak. No, they stood there watching her for a good few minutes until the youngest girl burst into copious tears and she knew that the game was up.

A woman she presumed to be a relative hurried quickly to their side and then another woman and another, watching and pitying.

'Miss Davenport let Mr Clairmont kiss her hand and she was standing close. Too close. She is after all betrothed to Lord Wilcox-Rice and I am certain that he would not like this.'

'Hush, Miriam, hush.' Another woman now came to their side, and the voice of reason and restraint might have swayed resolve had the older sister not also begun to sniff.

The whispers of interest began quietly at first, spreading across the ballroom floor like the ripples in a still summer pond after a large stone was thrown in carelessly. Wider and wider the curiosity spread, the fascination of intrigue shifting the weight of anger away from sympathy.

Her father's face was pale as he came towards her and there was a violent distaste on John's as he did not. Lillian saw her Aunt Jean frown in worry and heard the music of the orchestra wind into nothingness.

The sounds of ruin were not loud!

The colours of ruin were not lurid!

They were bleached and faded and gentle like the touch of her father's arm against her own, his fingers over hers, protective and safe.

'Come, Lillian,' he said softly, 'I shall take you home.'

Chapter Twelve

Luc left the Billinghurst town house and walked through the night, deep in his own thoughts as to what he should now do.

Lord, what might have happened had he stayed? He would have kissed her probably, kissed her well and good, and be damned with the whole effort of crying off.

'God help me.' The strain of it all made him breathe out heavily as he turned into a darkened alley affording a quick way back to his rooms.

Would Lillian have slapped his face and demanded an apology?

He could not risk it. Not yet. Not before she had had a chance to know his character and make her own choice as to whether she might want something more.

He swore again. He had always been a man who had carefully planned his life and made certain that the framework of his next moves were in place before he ventured on.

But here…he did not know what had just happened. How had he lost control so badly that he would risk her reputation on a whim?

In retrospect the full stupidity and consequences of his actions were blatantly obvious.

Lillian had not looked happy. She had not caught at his hand to hold him back, glancing instead towards the others in the room, towards her fiancé and her father, as her eyes had filled with tears.

How could he have got the whole thing so very, very wrong? Why the hell had he risked it all, anyway? Anger began to build. He was a colonial stranger with little to recommend him and a woman who sat at the very pinnacle of a society making much of material possessions would hardly welcome his advances in such a very public place.

'*If you kiss me here, I shall be ruined.*' Had she not said that to him as she had drawn back? Ruined by his reputation, ruined by his lack of place here, ruined by the fact that he had never truly fitted in anywhere save the wilds of Virginia with its hard honest labour and its miles of empty space.

Lord, he had lost one wife to the arms of another man because he had never understood just exactly what it meant to be married. Commitment. To stay in one place. Time. To nurture a relationship and sustain it even in the hours when nothing was easy. The example of his own parents' marriage was hardly one to follow and his uncle had never taken a wife at all.

He had never understood the truth of what it was that made people stay together through thick and thin, through the good times and the bad. Indeed, incomprehension was still the overriding emotion that remained from the five years of his marriage.

A noise made him turn and three men dressed in black stood behind him. His arm shot out to connect with the face of the first one, but it was too late. A heavy wooden baton hit him on the temple and he crumpled, any strength in his body leached into weakness.

As he fell he noticed a carriage waiting at the end of the alley, and he knew it to be the Davenport conveyance. For a second he was heartened that perhaps they were here to save him, but his hopes were dashed as a heavy canvas sack was placed over his head.

'The woman said to take him to the docks and that a man would meet us there.'

The woman?

She?

Lillian?

As the dizzy spinning unreality thickened he welcomed the dark whirl of nothingness, for it took away the bursting pain in his head.

Lucas Clairmont did not come as Lillian thought that he would. He did not come the first morning or the second and now it was all of five days past and every effort her father had made to find him had been fruitless. A man who had walked from the ballroom and out into the world, leaving all that was broken behind him.

He was not in his rooms in London and neither Lord Hawkhurst nor the St Auburns had any idea as to where he had gone. She knew because her father had spent the hour before dinner in her room explaining every ineffective endeavour he had made in locating the American.

'It is my fault all this has happened,' he said solemnly, running his fingers through what little was left of his hair. 'I pushed you into something untenable and your mind has lost its way.'

This melodramatic outburst was the first thing that had made Lillian smile since they had left the Billinghurst ball.

'I think it is more likely my reputation that is lost, Father.'

Ernest Davenport stood, the weight of the world so plainly on his shoulders and the heavy lines on his face etched in worry.

'I don't think Wilcox-Rice will forgive you. Even his sister is making her views about your transience well known.'

'I did not wish to hurt them.'

'But you did.'

No careful denial to make her feel better. She imagined the Wilcox-Rice family's perception of her with a grimace.

'And the worst of it is that you did it all for nothing.

I do not now know, daughter, that you will ever be married. I do not think that avenue of action is open to you after this.'

'But you will support me…' Fear snaked into the empty sound of her voice.

'Jean says that I should not. She says that you are very like your mother and that your lustful nature has been revealed.'

'No. That's not true, Father.'

'Everyone is speaking of us. Everyone is remembering Rebecca in a way that I had thought forgotten. We are now universally pitied, daughter. A family cursed in relationships and fallen from a lofty height.'

'All for a kiss on the back of my hand?'

'Ah, much more than that, I think. At least here in this room between us I would appreciate it if you did not lie.'

She remained silent and he inclined his head in thanks, honesty a slight panacea against all that had been lost.

'I think a sojourn in the north might be in order.'

'To Fairley Manor?' The same place as her mother had been banished to.

Her father's face crumpled and he drew his hands up to cover the grief that he did not wish her to see, and in that one gesture Lillian realised indeed the awful extent of her ruination and the folly of it.

'If you could find Lucas Clairmont, I am certain—'

Ernest dropped his hands and let irritation fly. 'Certain of what? Certain that he will marry you? Certain that this will be forgotten? Certain that society will forgive the lapse in judgement of someone whom they looked up to as an example of how a young woman should behave? You do not understand, do you? If it had been some other less-admired daughter, then perhaps this might have blown over, might have dissipated into the forgotten. But for all your adult life you have been lauded for manners and comportment. Lillian Davenport says this! Lillian Davenport does that! Such a stance has made you enemies in those who have not been so admired and they are talking now, Daughter, and talking loudly.'

She stayed silent.

'Nay, we will pack up the townhouse and retire to Fairley. At least there we can regroup. Jean, Patrick and Daniel will of course accompany us with the Christmas season almost here.'

Lillian's heart sank anew.

'And then we will see what the lay of the land is and make our new plans. Perhaps we could have a trip somewhere.'

So he would not abandon her after all. She laid her fingers across his.

'Thank you, Father.'

He drew her hand up to his mouth and kissed the back of it, a gesture she had not seen him perform since before her mother had left and the small loyalty of it pierced her heart.

When he was gone she pulled out a drawer in her writing desk and found a sheet of paper. She could not just leave such a silence between her and John and Eleanor Wilcox-Rice. With a shaking hand she began to apologise for all the hurt that she had caused them; when she had finished she placed the elegant gold-and-diamond ring in its box next to the note, pushing back relief. She would have it delivered in the morning. At least in the vortex of all that was wrong she was free of this one pretence.

Lucas Clairmont was gone. Back to America, perhaps, on a ship now heading for home? He had not contacted her, had not in any way tried to make right the situation between them.

Ruined for nothing!

The mantra tripped around and around in her head, a solemn and constant reminder of how narrow the confines of propriety were, and how completely one was punished should no heed be taken of convention.

Lord, she could barely believe that this was now the situation she would be in…for ever? Even the maid bustling into the room failed to meet her eyes, stiff criticism apparent in each movement.

Lunch that afternoon was a silent drawn-out affair, each person skirting around the disaster with particular carefulness.

Her youngest cousin Patrick was unexpectedly the one who remained the kindest, setting out all his *faux pas* across the years with an unrivalled honesty.

'It is an unfair world, Lillian, when women are disadvantaged for the actions of a cad. If Luc Clairmont should walk through this door right now, I would bash his head in.'

'Please, Patrick.' Jean's protests fell on deaf ears.

'And then I would demand retribution, though God knows in what form that might take, given his light purse—'

'I think your mother would prefer to hear no more.' Her father's voice was authoritative and Patrick stopped, the loud tick of the clock in the corner the one sound in the room.

'The Countess of Horsham's good opinion that no American is to be trusted has come to pass,' her aunt continued after a few moments. She lifted her kerchief and wiped at her watering eyes. 'And now we shall have no trip to Paris. For the wedding gown,' she qualified, noticing the puzzlement of the others.

'I should think that the lack of a shopping excursion is the least of our worries,' Ernest said, waiting as the servant behind reached over to remove his empty plate. 'But if we are to have any hope of weathering this disaster, we also need to put what is past behind us and move on.'

'How?' Jean returned quickly. 'How is it that we should do that?'

'By the simple process of never mentioning Lucas Clairmont's name again.'

Her aunt was quick to agree and Patrick followed suit. 'And you, Lillian?' her father said as he saw her muteness. 'How do you feel about the matter?'

'I should like to forget it, too,' she answered knowing that in a million years she would never do so, his pointed lack of contact a decided rejection of everything she had hoped for.

But as the days had mounted and the condemnation had blossomed, even amongst those who had no reason to be unkind, anger had crawled out from underneath hurt.

Why had he followed her into the dim privacy of the alcove if all he meant to do was leave her? Surely his actions had not been that mercenary?

Lilly. The way he had said her name, threaded with the emotion of a man whose control was gone, and whose touch had burnt the fetters off years of restraint, leaving her vulnerable. Exposed.

Her father's voice interrupted her reveries.

'We will leave for Fairley in the morning and shut the house here until the end of January. Some of the servants will stay to complete the process before they come on to us. If we are lucky this…incident may not have filtered out to the country and perhaps we may even entertain on a smaller scale. I hope, Patrick, that you in particular will not find the sojourn too quiet.'

Lillian gritted her teeth, though she was hardly in a position to remind her father of her own need for some company. The winter stretched out in an interminable distance: Christmas, New Year, Twelfth Night and Epiphany. All celebrations that she would no longer be a part of, her newly purchased gowns hanging in the wardrobe for no reason.

As the terrible reality of her situation hit her anew she pushed back her plate and asked to be excused. The eyes of her family slid away from her agitation, another sign of all that she had cost them in her error, for the invitations that had once strewn the trays were now dried up, and the few that pertained to a time in the future cancelled by yet another missive.

Her entire family had become *personae non gratae* and she had not stepped a foot outside the house in all of five days. Even the windows overlooking the park had been out of bounds—she often saw curious folk looking up and pointing.

Poor Lillian Davenport. Ruined.

Suddenly she could not care. She could not hide for ever. She was twenty-five, after all, and hardly a woman who had been caught in flagrant *déshabillé*.

Pulling on her heavy winter coat, her hat and her gloves, she called for the maid and the carriage to be ready to leave.

'I am not certain that the master—' The girl stopped when she noticed her expression. 'Right away, miss.'

Within the hour she was at her modiste trying on a dress she had ordered many weeks ago and Madame Berenger, the dressmaker, was polite enough not to ask anything personal, preferring instead to dwell on the fit and the form of the gown.

'It is beautiful on you, Miss Davenport. I like the back particularly with the low swathe across the bodice.'

Turning to the mirror, Lillian pretended more interest in the dress than she felt because a group of women she recognised had entered the shop.

An awkward silence ensued and then a whispering.

'It is her.'

'Has she seen us?'

Lillian tried not to react, though the hands of the modiste had stopped pinning the hem as though waiting for what might occur next.

'Perhaps now is not a good time to be here.' Christine Greenley spoke loudly, but the young assistant who had rushed to attend to the new arrivals assured her that there were seamstresses ready to help them.

'That may very well be the case, but will Miss Davenport be here long?' Lady Susan Fraser was not so polite. 'I should not wish to have to speak to her.'

No more pretence as silence reigned, the sound of a pin falling on to the wooden floor louder than it had any need to be.

Lillian thanked the woman kneeling before her and picked up the skirt of her gown so that she would not harm the fragile needlework. 'Please do not leave on my account, Lady Fraser, for I have finished.' The walking distance seemed a long one to the welcomed privacy of the curtains in the fitting room, her ingrained manners even giving her the wherewithal to smile.

Behind the velvet curtains her hands shook so much that she could barely remove the garment; when she looked at herself in the mirror it was like seeing a

stranger, eyes large from the weight she had lost in the
past week and dark shadows on her cheeks. Taking three
deep breaths, she prayed for strength, her maid's shy call
on the other side of the curtain heartening her further.

'Can I help with the stays, Miss Davenport?' she
queried, her face full of worry when Lillian bade her
enter and her fingers were gentle as she pulled the boned
corset into position and did up the laces.

When they came from the room the group was still
there however, the oldest lady stepping into her path as
she tried to leave.

'I am sorry for your plight, Miss Davenport.'

Her plight. Just what was she to say to that?

'Thank you.' Her words were a ludicrous parody of
good manners. Ever the gracious lady even in ruin!

'But at twenty-five you really ought to have known
better.'

'Indeed I should have.' Another inanity.

'If I could offer you some advice, I would say to go to
Wilcox-Rice cap in hand and beg his forgiveness! With a
little luck and lots of genuine apology, perhaps this situation could be remedied to the benefit of all those involved.'

'Perhaps it may.'

*Perhaps you should mind your own business.
Perhaps you should know that your son has proposi-
tioned me many a time in a rude and improper manner.*

Layers.

Of truth. One on top of the other and all depending
on the one beneath it.

And Luc Clairmont. What was his truth? she wondered, as she walked out on to the pavement, carefully avoiding meeting the eyes of anyone else before entering the waiting carriage and glad to be simply going home.

Lucas awoke to the sound of water, the deepness of ocean waves, the hollow echo of sea against timber and wind behind canvas sails. He was in the hull of a ship! Trying to swallow, he found he could not, his mouth so dried out that it made movement impossible.

An older man sat on the table opposite watching him.

'Ye are thirsty no doubt?'

Luc was relieved when the fellow stood and gave him a drink. Brackish water with a slight taste of something on the edge of it! When he lifted his hands to try to keep on drinking, he was pleased that his captors had not thought to bind him. The rattle of chains, however, dimmed that thought as he saw heavy manacles locked on his ankles.

'Where are we?' His voice was rough, but at least now he could speak.

'My orders were ye are not to be told anything.'

Luc attempted to glean from his fob watch some idea of the time, but the silver sphere was gone. Gone, like his boots and his jacket and cravat. Glancing across at a porthole at the far end of the cabin, he knew it to be still dark.

A few hours since they had taken him? Or a whole

day? He had no way of determining any of it. His head ached like the devil.

'You hail from Scotland?' He tried to make the question as neutral as he possibly could, tried to get the man talking, for in silence he knew he would learn nothing at all.

'Edinburgh, and before that Inverness.'

'I'd always meant to go north, but never did. Many say it to be a very beautiful land.'

'Aye, that it is. After all this—' he gestured around him '—I mean to go back, to live, ye understand.'

'If you help me off this ship, I could give you enough money to buy your own land.'

The other frowned. 'Ye are rich, then?'

'Very.'

The Scotsman eyed him carefully as if weighing up his options, the pulse in his throat quickening with each and every passing second. The sly look of uncertainty was encouraging.

'Are you a good judge of men?' Luc's question was softly asked.

'I like to think I am that, aye.'

'Then if I told you I am an innocent man who has done nothing wrong at all, would you believe me?'

The answer was measured.

'Any murderer could plead innocence should his life depend on it, but I've yet to see a man brought to this ship in the middle of the night who has not walked on the shady side of the law.'

Luc smiled. 'I would not expect you to do anything more than to look away for five minutes after unlocking these chains.' He gestured to the manacles at his ankles.

'I'd be a dead man if I did that.'

'Throw them overboard after me, then, and say that I jumped in.'

'Only a fool would attempt to swim while bound.'

'A fool or a desperate man?'

Silence filled the small cabin.

'When?' One small word imbued with so much promise!

Luc answered with a question of his own. 'Where are we headed?'

'Down to Lisbon.'

'Through the Bay of Biscay?'

'We have already sailed through those waters and have now turned south.'

'The warmer currents, then, off the coast of Portugal? If I jumped, I'd have a chance.'

'And my money?' The thread of greed was welcomed.

'Will be left at the Bank of England in Thread-needle Street, London, under my name.'

'Which is?'

'Clairmont. Lucas Clairmont. You could claim it when you are next back in England and then leave the ship for your hometown.'

'If ye die during this mad escape, I cannae see much in it for me.'

'Go to Lord Stephen Hawkhurst and tell him the

story.' Luc pulled his wife's ring from his finger and placed it on the ground in front of him, the gold solid and weighty in the slanting shaft of light from the porthole. 'I swear on the grave of my grandmother that he will pay you five hundred pounds for your trouble, no matter what happens to me.'

When a cascade of expletives followed Luc knew that he had him. Still, there was more that he might be able to learn.

'Who brought me on to this ship?'

'Three fellows who paid the captain for your passage. There was some talk of a woman who wanted ye gone from England if memory serves me well.'

Closing his eyes against the stare of the other, he tried to focus and re-gather his strength whilst thanking the James River for its lessons in swimming from one wide edge of it to the other.

Not Davenport money, he hoped. Not Lillian regretting her intimacy in the alcove at the Billinghurst ball, a dangerous stranger who would be menacing to her? A few pounds and an easy handover! No, for the very life of him he could not see Lillian ever performing an illegal act no matter what duress she might be under. Her aunt Jean, then? Lord, that made a lot more sense. Perhaps he was on the same ship she had bought a passage on for him, though he knew the paper in his pocket to be gone.

Already the man had brought the key from the table and unlocked the manacles. The chains fell limply around his ankles as he stood, towering over his shorter captor.

'What usually happens to those you take on the ship under the cover of darkness?'

'At a rough guess I'd say Lisbon would be the last place they ever saw in this life.'

The choice was made. Luc stripped off his shirt and tied it about his waist. He wished he could have picked up the wooden chair near the table and dashed it to pieces, taking the largest piece as ballast. But he did not dare to, for fear the noise would attract others who would not be as willing to barter.

'How do I leave the ship?'

'If you follow me, I will show you, but be quiet mind.' Lifting the chains, the Scotsman muffled their sound in the folds of his jacket as Luc followed him out into the darkness.

Chapter Thirteen

The tapestry in Lillian's hands was almost finished, an intricate design of fish and fowl wrought in the tones of grey and cream. The belated completion of half-finished projects such as this had been one of the positive things to come out of her enforced isolation and other embroideries still to be done lay in the basket at her feet.

Two weeks now since she had had any word from Lucas Clairmont. Fourteen days since her life had been changed completely by a man who had never wanted anything more than a dalliance. She hated him for it, and hated too the sheer and utter waste of effort it took to loathe him, a depression of spirit all that was left of wonder. From love to hate in fourteen days, tripped in an instant into a ruin she could barely comprehend.

Tears pooled behind her eyes and she willed them away, the picture before her blurring in sadness, though a commotion at the front door made her stand, voices shouting and the raised anger of her father and cousin. Another voice too, lower, familiar, the sound of a tussle and running feet.

'Lucas?' His name was snatched from her lips in a whisper as she ran, through the blue drawing room and into the hall, threads of grey and cream trailing in her wake.

Blood was everywhere, across Luc Clairmont's nose and eyes swelling shut under the fist of her cousin and his friend and he was not fighting back, the crack of his head as he fell on the marble leaving him dazed upon the floor.

'What is happening?' Her voice. Loud in the ensuing silence.

'He deserved it.' Patrick's explanation, the grazes on his fists bleeding anew even as he wiped them against the white linen of his shirt.

Did he? Does he? The question flared in her eyes as she stood between her father and her cousin, the opened door of the house letting in the stares of those servants who worked the gardens and also the wet of the driving western rains. She did not come forwards. She could not, two weeks of anger and hurt unresolved even in his re-appearance and a stiffening distance widening between them.

When he coughed and his amber eyes hardened before sliding away from her own, she knew that she had lost the chance of atonement, the feelings that had been between them withered into the unknown, two strangers brought to this place by circumstances that now seemed almost unbelievable.

She did not understand him, had never known who he was or what he wanted, an outlander who had strode into her life with the one sole purpose of disrupting it. And still was!

Her father's distress added to her own and with a sob she turned away, the silence left behind her telling. Lucas Clairmont did not call her back or try to stop her, the sound of her running feet against marble the only noise audible save for the frantic beating of her heart.

An hour later her father knocked on the door. He had changed his clothes, she saw, his shirt removed for a clean fresh one and his jacket and cravat in place.

Very formal for a country evening and no guests expected. Her mind began to turn.

'Lucas Clairmont would like to speak to you.'

'I do not think—'

'He is in the blue drawing room and I have told him you will be down immediately.'

Her glance went to his, but she could learn nothing there. 'I can see no point in prolonging what we both know will be the outcome of any meeting, Father.'

'You need to hear him out, Daughter. I have told him that after you have seen him he must leave and he has given me his word that he will.'

Still another barb to her heart! One last meeting. One final goodbye. Her fingers threaded through the hair that had fallen from its place beneath the shell comb at her nape and she tucked the strands back.

'Very well. I will be down in five minutes.' Her father's relief at her decision was faintly irritating, but she would not change or tidy herself up further. She would not stand there to be dismissed with her heart on her sleeve, and the weight of a ruined reputation between them. This was his fault every bit as much as hers and she would be the first to let him know it.

He looked worse than he had done an hour ago, new wounds upon his left cheek and fresh blood encrusted around the nails of the hand that she could see.

'Lillian.'

A sign, for he had seldom before called her that. There was flat anger in his glance.

'Your father has told me of the circumstances that have brought you and your family here and I would like to say that I am sorry—'

She could not let him finish. 'There is absolutely nothing to be sorry about, sir. We erred and we will pay. Society's rules are most explicit in that regard and any apology you might now wish to ply me with is by far and away too late.' The brisk distance in her voice pleased her, made her stronger.

'The price perhaps for you personally is rather steep and in that regard I would like to offer—'

'Oh, please—if it is something more permanent that you now feel compelled to tender, know that I should never accept it.'

He frowned, but remained silent, his hands now

firmly jammed in a jacket borrowed from her father. She recognised the cut of cloth and colour. Too small on him, the seams straining at the stitching on his side. His lack of argument fortified her.

'We barely know each other and what little we are cognisant of has resulted in disaster. My reputation is as ruined as your face! A truce of sorts! Surely now we should own up to what was never meant to be.'

'You would give up that easily?' His voice broke any polite restraint that she thought to hold on to.

'Give up what, sir? You are a mystery to me. A man who flirts with the affairs of the heart with no true understanding of what it all means. I trusted you, Mr Clairmont. I thought that you may have cherished what I had so senselessly offered, but you did not and then I understood. You are a gambler, a stranger, a liar and a cheat. It could never have worked between us, never, for I, unlike you, feel a certain responsibility to the titles I have inherited and to the rules and regulations that govern this land.'

'So in effect what you are saying is that I am not rich enough for you, Miss Davenport, not as well born as you have come to expect, and that that does matter?' The swollen flesh around his lips made the words slurred, a small vulnerability that she did not wish to notice.

'I am saying that you should go. That we should place this…madness into the slot to which it belongs.'

'Untenable?'

'Exactly.' Lillian's fervour broke as he looked up at

her and the word wobbled into a silence caught between then and now.

Then there was a chance and now there was not.

'And you would have no wish to know why I was away from London for these past weeks?'

'I would not. It is beyond the time for excuses and explanations and nothing you could say would make me believe that you did not realise that I was so badly compromised when you left the Billinghurst ball.'

'Nothing?' The word was phrased in a way she could not quite understand. 'I see.'

'I am glad that you do.' She shook her head, and tried to push back a rising grief. This was it. He would leave, hating her. Biting her top lip, she whirled around and made for the door, ignoring his plea to stop as she flew up the stairs and away.

Ernest Davenport read the documents laid out on his desk, the lawyer David Kennedy watching him from across the library with interest.

'So you are telling me that the man, far from being a pauper, has a series of large estates in Virginia and enough money to buy me out five times over?'

'Even that may be a conservative estimate.'

'You are also saying that this proposal of marriage comes with the distinct proviso of allowing none of this information to be leaked to my daughter should I choose to accept it.'

'Well, not you personally, you understand. This is not

the dark ages where a recalcitrant daughter is dragged screaming to the altar, after all. But I put it to you that your daughter's reputation had been…sullied and that this is the quickest and most beneficial way of making certain she is once again accepted back into society. I would also say that my client is most anxious that the lady not marry him just for his money, which accounts for the secrecy.'

'Why would he do this? Why would Lucas Clairmont want a betrothal to a woman who has much reason to hate him?'

'The motives of clients are something in my fifteen years at the bar I have never yet truly understood, sir. I am but the messenger, the simple emissary of news and deeds.'

'You are also held by a retainer, I should imagine?'

'That is correct, but I never accept a client without express knowledge of the honour of his character.'

'So you are saying he is not a charlatan?'

'I am, sir. I would also say that, as a father myself, I should be very cautious about turning down such a fortune.'

'Indeed.'

'My client also has a desire to have this union quickly completed.'

'How quickly?'

'It is my client's hope that Miss Davenport would be his bride by the beginning of next week. To that effect he has procured a special licence enabling the marriage to take place anywhere and at any time.'

Ernest lifted his pen, the nib carefully inked as he bent to it.

'Tell him that she agrees. Tell him that the wedding shall take place in the chapel here at Fairley Manor and tell him that if he hurts her again I will seek him out and kill him.'

'I shall relate each word to him, sir.' A small sense of the absurd was just audible.

'You do just that, Mr Kennedy.'

'You did wha-aa-at?'

'I accepted Mr Clairmont's proposal of marriage on your behalf, Lillian, because I think as a parent it is the only wise and proper thing to do.'

'Proper? Wise? He is a pauper and a liar, let alone a gambler. Are you telling me that you are happy to place the very future of Fairley into the hands of a man who will in all likelihood bleed it to death?'

'I am.'

'You are mad, Father. You cannot mean to do this, to tie our fortune to one who has proven to be so very untrustworthy.'

'I think, Lillian, that you besmirch his character too harshly. I think if you could find it in yourself to look upon this match as something that might indeed be of benefit to you both—'

'No!'

'The licence has been procured and the wedding is set for Monday.'

Monday for wealth
Tuesday for health
Wednesday the best day of all…

The ditty of days to marry turned in her head like some macabre promise.

'I do not believe this. Is he blackmailing you or threatening you in some way?' The horrible realisation made Lillian feel faint. This was not her father. This was not the careful and prudent man who would cut off his right arm rather than let the estate of Fairley Manor pass into the hands of an unsatisfactory groom.

'If he were, I should instruct you to turn him down.'

'And if I do just that, regardless?'

'Then we shall be for ever marooned here in Hertfordshire, neither a part of society or of village life because of your one unmindful mistake.'

Her mistake! The sacrifice of herself or of her family?

'If you force me into this travesty, Father, I will not forgive you for it and I will never understand it.'

'I beg to disagree, Daughter, for honestly in time I think that you will.'

She made no real effort with her wedding gown. In fact, at the very last moment she chose to wear a cream organza gown from her last Season because the new dress from Madame Berenger suggested an exertion that she felt far from making. In her hands, however, she held fragrant white winter daphne from the Fairley glasshouse because a small part of her could not quite abandon all form of good taste.

Lucas Clairmont stood at the top of the aisle watching her. She had not seen him since she had stormed away from him and the bruises were today a lurid green and yellow, his left eye still largely swollen. The way he held his right hand against his ribs also suggested substantial pain. His whole life seemed to tilt between contretemps, she thought, never settling into the easier peace of a comfortable and gentlemanly existence.

The tears that had not been far from her eyes all week banked yet again, the differences between them boding ill for any future they might be able to fashion.

The guests on her side of the chapel were packed into the pews with standing room only at the back. On his side, however, two couples sat. The St Auburns and Lord Stephen Hawkhurst, accompanied by a very old man.

Concentrating on the vase of flowers on a table behind the font, she noted them to be aged white carnations, some relative's clumsy touch evident in the overdone blooms and the fussy paper decorations around all the pews. She wanted to rip them away as she walked, but her dress was taking all of her attention, the wide skirt requiring a certain walk so that the material did not snag on the overhangs of the oak seats.

When the music stopped she stopped too, beside her husband-to-be, his clothes today surprisingly well tailored. Had Lord Hawkhurst leant him a frockcoat? she wondered, and then dismissed the whole thought.

It did not matter what he wore or how he looked. It did not matter that today he had made an effort with his attire she had not seen him make before. Perhaps he felt with the windfall of her dowry he had to be more careful to fit in, though when she took a quick peep at him he hardly looked overawed by a congregation of people far and away above him in rank, position and finances.

Even with his cuts and bruises he looked…confident. A man in the very place that he wanted to be!

Would she ever understand him? Would he ever know just how much he had hurt her? Her father obviously had some idea, the worry on his face making him look old and tired.

The clergyman raised his Bible. 'We are here today to marry Lucas Morgan Clairmont and Lillian Jewell Davenport.'

Lillian Clairmont! As the service continued the words that the priest wanted from her were difficult to say.

'…to love and to cherish from this day forward until death do us part.'

Such an empty troth! She wondered why an omnipotent God did not smite the church with an earthquake or a shower of hail or at the very least inveigle his man to question the intent. But the clergyman droned on as if it had oft been his misfortune to marry a less-than-jubilant bride.

Nothing about this wedding was anything like she had imagined it would be; when Lucas Morgan Clairmont reached out for her hand and slid the ring on her finger, it seemed like just another extension of an awful day.

The wedding band was a lurid yellow gold and embossed with a heavily set ruby, a ring that worked on the premise that bigger was better and that comfort was barely to be considered. No cheap piece either, but one fashioned only with the wish to impress.

Had he stolen it? Had he won it in a game of cards? She tucked her hand away into the folds of her skirt and wished he had not given her such an obvious piece. In contrast, the band she had given him was of classic plain gold and engraved with their initials and a date.

When the priest intimated that the bride and groom might now kiss, Lucas merely shook the suggestion away and turned for the door, leaving her to follow in his wake as she tried not to catch the eyes of all those present on her side of the church. The wedding dress bumped against her legs as she hurried to keep up.

Lord, when the hell would this be over? Luc thought, as he tried to maintain a peace of mind that he had not felt in all the days since being back in England.

He had hit the water with a shock of fear, ten miles off a coast he had no knowledge of and the black ink of ocean stretching for ever. It was only for Lillian that he had kept going, stroke after stroke through the currents and the endless waves, the sea in his eyes and nose and throat. Yet now? His wife looked as though she hated him and her aunt Jean Taylor-Reid behind gave the impression of a woman seeing a ghost back from the dead.

Luc breathed out, wishing he might confront Lillian's aunt with his accusations and knowing at this minute that he just could not.

Lord, what was it he was doing? He had made the mistake of marrying badly once before and the first thrall of exaltation he had felt when Lilly had agreed to marry him was now fading into apprehension.

He hated weddings, hated the empty promise of them and the forced joviality that was almost always accompanied by a large dollop of uncertainty.

At least at his last wedding the bride had worn a dress that let him get near her and the words she had given were edged in hope rather than anger. Yet look where that had got him!

Lillian had barely glanced at him and had snatched her hand from his as soon as the ring was placed on her finger, the special licence he had purchased suddenly looking like a reckless thing.

Better perhaps to have taken her professed dislike of his character at face value and departed for America, where his lands and houses waited and the living was easy.

Easy? He could not have said that even three months ago with the guilt of Elizabeth crippling him and a drinking problem he could do little about.

Lilly with her pale goodness seemed to have cured him, made what before was impossible, possible. A woman he respected and liked. No, he could not just walk away.

'You look pensive, Luc?'

Hawk offered him a glass of lemonade and he took it.

'I was thinking that my bride doesn't look particularly happy...'

'Nat said that Cassie was as miserable at their wedding.'

'She ran away from him the next day, remember?'

Stephen smiled. 'I had forgotten about that.'

A flash of cream to one side of the room had them both turning.

'It seems that Alfred has made himself known to your new spouse. How long do you think it will be before she realises my uncle is somewhat soft in the head?'

'About now, I'd say,' Luc interjected. 'He seems to be trying to extract my wedding ring from her finger. Perhaps you could persuade him not to, Hawk.'

But before either man had moved Lillian had solved the problem completely. With little fuss she removed the band and handed it to him, watching as he held it up to the window for a better look at the jewel in the light.

'Well,' said Hawk, 'that's a first. Usually they run screaming from him.'

'She didn't wait to collect the ring back either,' Luc added as he watched her move on. 'Do you think she has any notion as to how much it is worth?'

'She is a lady of taste, Lucas. Of course she knows it and right down to the last copper farthing, if I had my guess.'

'Then why would she just leave it with him?'

'Your grandmother was never one known for her artistic eye.'

'She was given the piece by the Duke of Gloucester's mistress.'

'And it shows!'

Seen like that, Lucas felt the first twinge of uncertainty. 'I'll buy her another one, then.'

'I think the ring's the least of your worries, Luc. Your bride looks miserable.'

'She thinks I deserted her intentionally.'

'You didn't tell her about the kidnapping? Why the hell wouldn't you tell her that?'

When he remained quiet, Stephen swore.

'God. You think she had something to do with it…'

'No.' The word was said loudly and had people turning. He remembered back to the lies Elizabeth had told. Little lies at first and then bigger ones as he had struggled to understand her anger and her moods. From Lillian he could not weather lies.

When Nathaniel broke into the conversation by slapping him on the back and indicating that the speeches were just about to start, he was relieved. Tempering worry, he walked to the head of the room to stand next to Lily.

Her newly acquired husband had been conversing happily with his friends whilst she was struggling to keep a thinly held composure. The absurdity of their marriage just kept on escalating. He was enjoying himself whilst she was so plainly not, her ugly dress hampering all sense of confidence and the horrible wedding ring lost into the hands of an ancient simpleton.

Stephen Hawkhurst's uncle it was said when she had asked his identity, a man who had been a little simple for years. Her hand crept to a growing headache about her temple as the speeches she had been dreading were called for. What would Lucas Clairmont say? Or her father?

Was this the part when the whole affair erupted into the fiasco it truly was? Surreptitiously she looked around to see where her cousin Daniel stood and was glad to find him missing. At least that was one less thing to worry about! Patrick, however, seemed bent on shadowing her every move, whether from a stance of protection or a desire to flex his muscles again, she could not be sure. Outside the rain beat against the roof.

Happy be the bride the sun shines on…

Today all she could think of were rhymes that scoffed at any inherent hope she might try to muster.

Her father began the toasts, raising up his glass and waiting for silence. 'To the bride and groom,' he said eventually when the room was quiet, his eyes settling on her. 'May they enjoy a long and joyous life together!'

'And fruitful,' someone called out, a rumble of amusement rippling around the room.

Not from her, though! The crass reminder of what this night could bring was suddenly and terribly in Lillian's mind. Would Lucas Clairmont expect fruitful, knowing what he did? Could he in all conscience demand what it was she had offered less than an hour ago before a man of God, knowing her feelings about this charade?

To love and to cherish...

Such tiny words for all that they implied.

Goodness, she thought, fixedly staring at the floor as the lump of terror in her throat congealed...if he thought that I might... She chanced a quick glance at her husband and the brittle smile that he gave back did nothing to reassure her. No, the opposite, in fact, because in the amber light she caught a glimpse of the lust that *fruitful* engendered, a very masculine under-standing of all that a wedding night meant.

She shivered again and unexpectedly Lucas Clair-mont moved closer, the light wool in his blue frockcoat resting against the thin layers of silk and organza across her arm. As a measure of comfort? She hoped that he had meant it such, but was doubtful. Anne Weatherby and Cassandra St Auburn standing together across the room both smiled at her, a tinge of anxiety in their looks, and Lillian wished Eleanor Wilcox-Rice might have come, too, but of course in the circumstances she could not, the stiff letter she had had in answer to her own note implying the desire for no further correspondence. She smoothed down the growing crinkles in her dress as at-tention swung back to her husband, alarm setting her heart to racing at a pace she felt worried about as she saw that it was now his turn to reply.

'Please, Lord, let him speak with authority and honour.' The whisper of prayer hung in the empty corners of her pride.

Lucas paused for a moment as though thinking of what it was he wished to impart; when he did begin speaking, he sounded neither breathless nor nervous.

'Ernest Davenport has given me the pleasure of taking his only daughter's hand in marriage and I would like to thank him for his generosity.' Lillian wondered why her father looked away, a rising blush evident upon his cheeks. Had she missed something important? 'I have known Lillian…' He halted, as though he would have perhaps preferred to use Lilly, but had decided against it. 'I have known Lillian for only a short while, but in that time have come to realise that she has all the attributes of an admirable wife. So it is with great pride that I stand before you all as her groom today and thank you for your presence here.'

Nothing of love or respect or even friendship! Lillian worried her bottom lip as he continued. 'Please raise your glasses and drink to my wife.'

When her name echoed around the room she inclined her head in thanks, her eyes widening as Stephen Hawkhurst's uncle stood from the chair in which he sat.

'Your ring's been blessed, did you know?' he began. 'The fairies came before and sanctified your union. It is not often that this happens, in fact, I have not seen the little folk in years, not since my brother's wedding in the March of 1816 when they came…'

Lord Hawkhurst had reached his uncle by now and taken him by the arm, meaning to lead him away. Lillian noticed that he did so gently but the old man wasn't finished.

'Yours will be a happy and long marriage, I am certain of it…' But now his voice was distant, the mere echo of it lying in the silence of the room. Lucas, however, did not seem content to leave it at that as the first awkward titters of embarrassment and fluster began to flow.

'Lord Alfred Hawkhurst was a soldier who took a bullet in the head for his country in the second Peninsular campaign under Wellington. In doing so he saved twenty of his regiment from certain death and as a hero deserves at least compassion.'

The snickering stopped.

An old hero in the guise of a fool! Her wedding in the guise of a celebration! Her husband in the guise of a man who held honour above the easier pathway of saying nothing!

For the first time in weeks she liked Lucas Morgan Clairmont again and was heartened by it.

Chapter Fourteen

It was almost four o'clock and Lucas knew that the time had come to take his bride and go home to Woodruff Abbey, an hour and a half away on the Northern Road.

He had toyed with the idea of paying for a room at the Elk and Boar Inn, a point that broke the journey halfway, but with the indifference marking Lillian's face had decided that being cramped together in a small space might not be the wisest thing to do.

Indeed, he even wondered about the carriage ride and wished that Hawk and his uncle had made plans to stay at Woodruff until the morrow. Such a desperate thought made him smile and as he did so he caught his wife looking at him.

'If you are ready to leave, I thought we might go?'

'Go where?' Her astonishment gave him the impression that she had expected to stay at Fairley Manor.

'My home is in Bedfordshire. A place called Woodruff Abbey.'

'And it is yours?'

He could not help but hear the catch of surprise in her voice. 'I only recently came into the inheritance.'

The interest that crossed into her eyes was tempered by disbelief, the whole charade of whom and of what he was here in England mirrored in pale blue uncertainty.

He hoped that Lillian would not hate the Abbey, would not demand the perfection of Fairley, would not turn up her nose at the shabby beauty of a house that was coming to mean a lot to him.

Lord, let her like it!

The emptiness of his last few years made him swallow and he knew that he could not survive should this marriage prove as disastrous as his first.

Ernest Davenport, seeing their intent to leave, came up to speak, his eyes watering a little as he held the hand of his daughter.

'I shall journey to see you for Christmas, Lillian.'

Lucas noticed how his wife's fingers curled about that of her parent as if she was desperate not to let him go. 'If you would wish to come sooner…' she began, but Davenport stopped her.

'Nay, the first weeks in a new marriage are for you and your groom alone. But I would just speak to your husband privately, for a moment?'

Lillian made a show of bidding her remaining family goodbye as Luc walked to the window with her father.

'This unconventionality of telling my daughter little about the state of your finances will be obeyed by me only until I see you again in a fortnight. Do you understand?'

Lucas nodded. Davenport had kept his word thus far and he was thankful for it, but with Christmas less than two weeks away he knew that he was running out of time.

'And if I hear that there has been anything untoward happening…'

'I would never hurt your daughter.'

'Your lawyer gave you my message, then?'

'He did, sir.' Lucas remembered David Kennedy's less-than-flattering summation of Ernest Davenport's parting words.

'I notice that she is not wearing her wedding ring?'

'No, it is here in my pocket.' He had retrieved the band from Hawk's uncle once the old man had lost interest in it.

'It does not look like a piece that my daughter would be fond of. If I might offer you some advice, having it reset completely may be the wiser option.'

Lilly's father and Hawk felt the same way?

Luc felt a strange sense of kinship with the man opposite. He was, after all, a father just trying to do his best by his daughter.

'I shall certainly think about it, sir.'

Lillian shifted in her seat when the carriage began to slow almost two hours later, pulling off the road and slipping through intricate wrought-iron gates. It had been a silent trip to Woodruff Abbey as two of her maids had shared the space with them, the lack of privacy allowing nothing personal at all to be said and slanting rain the only constant noise of the journey. When they rounded the last corner, she saw that the house before them was like something from another century.

'It needs a lot of work,' Luc declared as he leaned across to look at it and Lillian thought she detected a hint of apology in his voice.

In the growing darkness she could only just make out the newly weeded verges around the circular drive and the piles of pruned branches heaped to one end of a low-lying addition. Could this have been where her husband had been in the last weeks? Trying to make something of his windfall?

'The lines of the building are beautiful.' In all her hurt she found herself reassuring him and was rewarded with a smile as a footman drew down the steps, Lucas's hand coming to assist her after he had alighted.

Lillian was surprised by the bareness of the place as they walked in, though there was a certain beauty in the ancient rugs and the few pieces of furniture that were on display. An old dog roused itself from beneath a table and stretched, before coming to see just who the new arrivals were and three long-haired cats watched them from a small sofa placed by the stairway.

'This is Royce, the mongrel,' her husband said as he bent to pat the dog, its tongue licking the inside of his palm with a considerable force. For Lillian, who had never had much contact at all with animals inside a house, the plethora of pets was alarming. 'He is at least fifteen years old, although Hope believes him to be older still.'

'Hope?'

Lord, she thought, the tale she had heard of his children ensconced in some house suddenly taking on a frightening reality.

'You will meet her and her sister tomorrow.'

Before she could answer an old man appeared, a similar-aged woman behind him pulling away the strings of a well-used apron as she too shuffled forwards.

'Mr Lucas,' she said, taking his arm with delight. 'You are back already?' Her glance took in them both. 'And with your lady wife, too?'

'Lillian Clairmont, meet Mr and Mrs Poole, my housekeeper and head butler.' The appellations seemed to please the older couple and she was astonished by the fact that her husband kept up such friendly terms with the serving staff that he would introduce them like equals. The Americans were odd in such ways, she surmised, giving the woman a polite but reserved smile.

'Well, I have your room ready, sir, and the eider-down I embroidered myself over the winter months is just this week finished, so no doubt you will be warm and toasty.'

Your room? Warm and toasty? These words implied exactly what Lillian did not wish to hear at all, though the small squeeze her new husband gave her kept her mute.

'I am certain everything will be well prepared, but as we are tired would it be possible to send up a tray with some food?'

Goodness, in England these words were never used to serving staff—they implied a great deal of choice on behalf of the paid attendants. As a new landlord and employer, Lucas Clairmont had a lot to learn. The sneaking feeling that he could well be getting duped with his household expenses also came to mind, though the couple before her did not, in all truth, look like a dishonest sort, but merely rather strange and doddery.

The same headache that she had been cursed with all day suddenly began to pound and despite everything she was pleased to be led upstairs by her husband and into a bedroom on the second floor.

It was a chamber like no other she had ever been in, bright orange curtains at the windows and a red and purple eiderdown proudly slung across a bed that was little bigger than a single one.

On a table were bunches of wildflowers in the sort of glass jar that jam was usually found in and beside that lay a pile of drawings. Children's drawings depicting a family in front of a house, two small girls in pink dresses before a couple holding hands.

'Charity likes to draw,' her husband explained, picking up the sheath of papers and rifling through them. 'I think she has a lot of talent.'

He held up another picture of the same black-and-white dog downstairs, though this time Royce sat in a field of wildflowers, the sun above him vividly yellow. With no idea at all of the stages of refinement in a child's artistic ability, Lillian had to admit to herself that it seemed quite well done. Indeed, the artist had exactly copied the slobbery mouth and the matted coat, though the angel complete with halo perched before it was an unusual addition.

'Charity always draws her mother in these things,' Lucas explained when he saw her looking. Finding the first drawing, he alerted her to the same angel balanced on the only cloud in the sky.

'Her mother was your first wife?'

He shook his head and the whole picture became decidedly murkier. 'No, their mother was my wife's sister.'

Lillian sat down. Heavily. 'You dallied with your wife's sister?'

'Dallied?' His amber eyes ran across her face, perplexity lining gold with a darker bronze. 'I did not know her at all.'

'I thought—they say you are their father. How could you not have known her?' Lillian no longer cared how her voice sounded, perplexity apparent in every word.

A deep laugh was his only answer. The first time she had heard him laugh since…when? Since he had held her in the drawing room in London and shaken away her feebly offered kiss. The chamber swirled a little, dizzy anger vying with horror as she realised well and truly that she was now married to a man who appeared to have absolutely no moral fibre. And that she still wanted him!

'The children are my wards. I am not their father, but their guardian.'

'Oh.' It was all that she could say, the rising blush of her foolish deduction now upon her face as he crossed the room to fill a glass of water from a pitcher and drank it.

'Do you want one?' he asked as he finished and when she nodded he refilled the same glass and handed it to her.

Married people shared beds and houses and glasses of water, she ruminated, and the thought made her suddenly laugh. A strange strangled sound of neither mirth nor sadness. She imagined that if she could have seen the expression on her face she might look a little like the baffled angel in Charity's drawings—a woman who found herself in a position that she could not quite fathom.

Unexpectedly a tear dropped down her cheek and Lucas moved forwards, his thumb tracing the path of wetness with warmth.

'I know that this is all different for you and that the house is not as you may have hoped it to be, but—'

She shook her head. 'It is not the house.'

'Me, then?'

She nodded. 'I do not really know you.' She refused to look at him as she said it, and refused to just stop there. 'And now this room with one bed between the two of us…'

'Nay, it is yours. Tonight I shall sleep elsewhere.'

The relief of that sentence was all encompassing, and she swallowed back more tears. She never cried, she never blushed, she had never felt this groundless shifting ambivalence that left her at such a loss, but here, tonight, she did not even recognise herself, a quivering mannerless woman who had made little effort with anyone or anything for the whole of her wedding day and was now in a room that looked like something out of a child's colourful fairytale.

And yet beneath everything she did not want her pale and ordered old life back, and it was that thought more than anything that kept her mute.

She looked as if she might crumple if he so much as touched her, looked like a woman at the very end of her tether and the fact that the water in the glass had stained the front of her cream bodice and gone unnoticed added further credence to his summations.

His new wife was beautiful, her cheeks flushed as he had never seen them before and her skirt pushed up at such an angle that he could glimpse her shins, the stockings that covered shapely ankles implying that the rest of her legs would be just as inviting.

The direction of his thoughts worried him and to take his mind off such considerations he took the wedding ring from his pocket and laid it in his hand.

'I retrieved this from Lord Alfred.'

She remained silent.

'Though I have had advice that the setting may not be quite to your taste?'

A look of sheer embarrassment covered her face. 'No, it is perfectly all right.'

Manners again, he thought, and it was on the tip of his tongue to insist otherwise when she stood and put out her hand.

'I am sorry for the careless way I treated your ring.'

She did not say that she liked it, he noticed, as he took her left hand into his own, the fingers cold and her nails surprisingly bitten down almost to the quick.

At the very end of her forefinger was a deep crescent-shaped scar, the sort of mark a knife would make, but he said nothing for fear of spoiling the moment as he slipped the band back upon her finger.

A sign that things could be good or a shackle that held her to him despite every other difference?

'How old was your wife when she died?' The question unsettled him, but he made himself answer.

'Twenty-four. Her name was Elizabeth.'

'And you met her in Virginia?'

'She was the daughter of an army general who was stationed near Boston.'

'Nathaniel said that she was killed in an accident?'

The anger in him was quick, spilling out even as he tried to take back the words. 'No. I killed her by my own carelessness. It was a rain-filled night and the path too difficult for a carriage.'

'Did you mean for her to die?' Lilly's voice was measured, the matter-of-factness within it beguiling.

'No, of course I didn't.'

'Then in my opinion it was an accident.'

Light blue eyes watched him without pity. Just an

accident. In her view. Perhaps she was correct? The hope of it snatched away his more usual all-encompassing guilt and he breathed out, loudly.

'Are you always so certain of things?' This was a side of her he had not seen before.

The answering puzzled light in her eyes reminded him so forcibly of the time that he had kissed her in London he had to jam his hands in his pockets just to stop himself from reaching out again.

Not now. Not yet. Not when she so plainly was frightened of him.

'Certain? I used to think I was such, but lately…' The shadows of the past week bruised her humour, and because of that he tried to explain even just a little of what lay unsaid between them.

'When I left London the night of the ball I had no notion that anyone had seen us, and I should like to explain just what happened next—' He stopped as she shook his words away.

'My ruination was as much my fault as it was yours. More, perhaps, for at least you had the foresight to stop it at a touch.'

'You wanted me to keep going?'

The very thought of it had the blood rushing to places that he knew would show and he turned. Lord, suddenly he wanted all the promise of a wedding night, all the whispers, soft words and touches, the burning pleasure of release and elation.

'I do not know…perhaps…?'

Given as a gift of honesty. The squeeze of relief in his heart made him giddy. Not at all like Elizabeth then, he thought, for she had seldom been truthful when it suited her not to be.

A knock at the door allowed the entry of two young maids who efficiently set out steaming dinners on trays at the table. A bottle of water was added to the fare just before they left.

'You do not drink wine?' she asked as they sat down to the supper.

'After the carriage accident I drank too much…'

'And then you met my cousin, whom you seem to dislike?'

Luc felt himself tense up. Lord, how was he to tell her anything, a woman who had been cocooned by a genteel and refined upbringing? He could see it in her skin, in the softness of her hands, in the worry of her eyes and in the shake of her voice. Tonight was her wedding night, damn it, and she could not wish to hear anything so sordid. Forcing a smile, he raised his glass to her. 'There is much in my life that has been more difficult than your own, and there are things that I have done that I am now sorry for.'

'Things?'

He laughed, more out of sheer unease than anything else, and hated the way her smile was dashed from her eyes.

'Things that I am not proud of now, but were at the time necessary.'

'To survive?'

He nodded. 'Survival here is a simpler process. Break the rules in England and you are banished. Break them in Virginia and you are left fighting for your life.'

'As you have been?' Her eyes deliberately ran across the scar on his neck. He saw the fear in them and his hand caught hers, his fingers running along the inside of her opened palm, stroking, asking.

For a chance, for a second chance, the softness of her skin against his just a small reminder of all that was different between them.

Lilly closed her eyes and felt. For this one moment in her wedding day she just felt what it was other brides might, the trail of his fingers evoking a thrall in her she had only ever known once before. With him.

Was this an answer?

An easy ending to everything that was different between them. A bride and groom thrown together not by love, but by ruin.

She knew nothing of his life or his beliefs, nothing of his family or his country or the things that he knew as right and wrong. If they made love here and now it would be just that, bodies touching where minds could never follow, a shallow knowledge of desire that had nothing to do with the heart.

When she pulled away he let her go and stood with his hands by his side, watching, a man of honour and constraint, but one with enough questions in his eyes to make her understand what it was he asked.

If not now, then when?

The fire of his appetite was easy to interpret. Such a masculine simplicity! For a second the very sincerity of it made her pause, no pretence or artifice, no false posturing at something else either.

Not love, but need, his man's body bristling with something she did not understand yet, but knew enough to be wary about.

'If you could be patient.'

He nodded stiffly, the bronze in his eyes brittle. All of a sudden the sheer and utter amazement of sharing a meal at night and alone was scintillating. Exhilarating.

No longer single, but married.

The very idea of it seeped through her body in an unexpected warmth, as her memory of the one kiss he had given her began to tug at a power deep inside. It overwhelmed her, this newness of being here, and she could barely take breath as a hot flush of what he might do to her again surfaced. Too raw. Too quick after such a day. A single trail of sweat ran between her breasts and the cream dress was not thick enough to hide what she knew with horror was suddenly on show.

Her nipples stood proud against the silk, pressing and swollen. What was it that a husband did to a wife in a marriage bed beneath the sheets under the cover of darkness?

She did not know. Had never known. Until now. Until

a knowledge that was as old as time itself began to wind itself through an aching anticipation, the thickening throb of her womanhood making her languid, heavy.

If he saw he did not say anything, a man who had spent the day balancing her unhappiness, her cousins' anger and her father's uncertainty like juggling balls as he tried to get through a wedding he could hardly want, either.

Her mind remembered Lord Hawkhurst's uncle's words. *A happy and long marriage?* She wished suddenly that she could be brave enough to ask right here and now of his movements across the last weeks and of his hopes for the future, but she did not want to in case the answers were nothing like the ones she needed to hear.

The longing in her body was replaced by a wooden fear of everything. Two strangers sharing a meal without any idea as to who each other was, their wedding clothes and rings only a ludicrous parody.

Just silence.

And then another sound.

'Mr Lucas. Mr Lucas.' A child's voice from afar and as the door was flung open a small dark-haired girl bolted into the room, stopping briefly as her eyes sensed Lillian's presence, but then regrouping.

'You are home again. Mrs Poole said that we should wait until the morrow, but—'

'We?' He looked around just as she did and there at the door stood a more timid child, hair so blonde it was almost silver and eyes a wide pale blue.

'Charity wanted me to wait, but she is so much slower I could not.'

The other child came forwards, a shy smile of gladness gathering on her lips.

'Charity and Hope, this is Lillian Clairmont.'

Hope smiled at her, but the other child looked away.

'We were married today at her country home of Fairley.'

'This is your ring?' Hope's finger traced the band of gold on the hand that held her.

'Indeed it is.'

'Look, Charity. Isn't it lovely?' the dark-haired girl exclaimed and the smaller child nodded.

'And the lady wore that…?' A thread of something akin to disappointment startled Lillian, although Lucas did not seem to notice any criticism.

'She did and she looked very beautiful.'

'I will wear lace and silk and a tiara when I get married and I will have flowers in my hair.'

The appearance of a harried-looking governess at the doorway curtailed the amusements.

'I am so very sorry, sir. The girls were told to stay in their room and I thought that they were there until I heard footsteps and followed the sound.'

'Please could you come and tuck us in? Please, Mr Lucas.'

He looked at the time. 'If you do not mind, Lillian, it is late and the girls…'

'Indeed,' she answered back, trying to keep her tone

light. 'They would obviously like you to settle them and I am very tired.'

He seemed to hesitate at that, as though he might have wanted to say more, but then thought again.

'Then I shall bid you goodnight.'

'Goodnight,' Hope parroted, and they were all gone, just the bustling sound of them receding into silence.

Lillian stared at the closed door with a growing amazement. Goodness, she thought, and turned to lift the lurid purple eiderdown around her shoulders, the quilting on the back of it catching her eye with the very fineness of detail.

A movement to one side of the room made her start as a large grey-and-white cat padded towards her.

'Shoo,' she said, but the word did not seem to change the animal's direction one bit as it lurched itself up on the bed, the sound of purring distinct and deep. Tentatively her hand went out, running across the thick fur, a quiet delight enveloping her.

'I said shoo,' she repeated, allowing the cat on to her lap even as she said it, the warmth of its body comforting in the cold of the evening. Soft paws pushed into her thighs, kneading the layers of silk and organza. Almost tickling.

The whole day had been a skelter of emotion. Up and down. This way, that way. Touching and distance. No true direction in any of it. She closed her eyes and breathed in, the ugly ring on her finger winking up at her with its bright deep red.

* * *

Damn, damn, damn, Luc thought, after he had tucked in the two children and gone back to his own room. The wilting ache of his body was as out of place here as his desperate attempt at ignoring the hard outline of Lillian's breasts against silk.

Take it slowly, he thought. Give her the time she wants!

'If you could be patient.'

But even now he wanted to go back, wanted the promise of what could be, wanted to see the beauty of what lay beneath her dress, her nipples puckered with yearning. But he could not.

Careful, he thought. Go carefully. The reason for his ordeal at sea still worried him and the truth was not as yet such an easy path to follow.

He had married Lilly to save her reputation and any other feelings that were as yet unresolved lingered in a place he had no wish to explore. Had she had any hand in his disappearance? Had Jean Taylor-Reid acted alone? Did the woman have any true idea of the danger she had placed him in? Perhaps she genuinely thought she had bought passage for him to the Americas, an easy way of dealing with a problem that was becoming more and more complex.

The whole puzzle of it made him swear and he was tempted to open the brandy standing on his desk. But he didn't.

He needed to trust Lilly and she needed to trust him. If he took her virginity in the guise of a man who was not exactly as he promised he was, he knew she would never forgive him.

Damn, he said again as the knowledge of what he could have just missed out on settled in his stomach like a stone.

Taking a drink of Mrs Poole's freshly made lemonade, he settled down to read the final part of Dickens's Bleak House, the title appropriate for all that he was feeling tonight.

Chapter Fifteen

'This hillock affords the best view of the place,' Lucas said as they stopped atop a cliff. 'I think it must have once been a river-bed, for the water has cut through the sandstone etching out the land. See, there is still the remains of a smaller stream.'

Lillian looked at where he was pointing. 'You have a good knowledge of geography.'

He shook his head. 'Rivers are the same anywhere. They divide the country with their own particular brand of frivolity and men must simply follow their course.'

'Like the river near where you live? The James, was it not?'

'And you have a good memory,' he returned before spurring his horse on and gesturing her to follow.

They had spent the morning wandering the wide lands of Woodruff Abbey, his attempt, she suspected, at keeping her busy and having enough space between them to make things…simple. No touching, no deeper conjectures, just the land and the choice of moving on once conversation foundered.

And yet she was enjoying the tour, enjoying the cold winter sun on her face and the exploration of an estate that was magnificent in its diversity. The caves they now stopped beside were mossed with lichen and carvings, sticks wedged as sentinels protecting angular sandstone facings.

This time he dismounted and came over to help her down. Having no other recourse but to accept, she waited as his hands came around her waist, her body sliding down the length of his until her toes met the ground.

Moving away as soon as she was stable, the material in his riding jacket strained across the breadth of his shoulders. Today he was neither the Lucas Clairmont who had kissed her in London nor the dangerous man at Fairley with blood on his face and anger in his eyes. The Lucas Clairmont of yesterday had disappeared, too, with his confidence and certainty. This man was gentler, more considerate, with no hint of demanding more than she would give him. A patient, self-controlled husband who had spent his wedding night alone!

She suddenly missed the man who would tease her and reach out unbidden, his golden reckless glance today well guarded, as if he was trying to be on his best behaviour.

Lillian's heart began to beat faster. Was that what he was doing? Nurturing patience?

'If you could be patient.' She had asked that of him yes-

terday. Had he retreated into trying? Warmth began to spread into the cold anger that the wedding had imbued, flushing the possibility of something very different.

'Jack Poole says these carvings have been here since before any written history.' His voice was tight, the facts given with a stiff correctness.

'So they don't really know who did them?' Sitting on the nearest rock, she hitched up her skirts to keep them from trailing in the dust.

'He says Viking travellers, thanes from the early part of the eighth century. People who crossed this part of England to battle the Saxon warriors fiercely defending themselves in the last free land of Wessex.'

His voice petered off as his eyes met her own, the bare facts of history irrelevant now in the growing silence. For the first time since she had met him she felt that she was in charge, the knuckles in his fist pressed white on the hand she could see, his wedding band glinting in the sun.

'An old history, then.'

He only nodded. A man who had probably reached the end of his patience!

'In which part of England did you live as a boy?'

'In the north-east,' he said obliquely. Telling her nothing.

'You seldom answer questions about yourself. I have noticed it.'

At that he laughed, but the sound of it was hard. 'Ask me anything.'

She pondered for a moment. 'Why did you steal the watch at Eton?'

'Anything but that.'

'Very well, then! How did you meet Nathaniel St Auburn and Stephen Hawkhurst?'

'At school. We were in the same year when we were all sent there at eleven and I was there for a good while. Holidays were also generally spent at St Auburn or Hawthorne Castle, Hawk's family seat in Dorset.'

'And what of your home? Your parents?'

'My father and mother were rarely home and when they were I stayed as far away as I could get.'

Lillian glanced up, this answer nothing like the others, a ring of truth and anger so desperately heard within it. But he did not look at her as he gazed across the wide valley, a few wildflowers even at this time of the year, caught in the change of seasons and the on-slaught of winter. Brittle and temporary! She knew just exactly how they felt.

'You were an only child?'

He nodded, but the honesty of a second ago was gone. Regretting his outburst probably, she thought, by the look of the muscle that rippled to one side of his cheek.

'And they did not follow you to America?'

'No.'

'Then who did you live with when you got there?'

'An uncle. My father's brother. A fine man by the name of Stuart Clairmont.' He shook his head as she went to speak again. 'Are you always this curious?'

'You are my husband. Spouses ought to be curious about each other.'

'Very well, then,' he returned. 'Tell me something about you that nobody else knows.'

He saw the way her lips tightened, her pale eyes searching his face for what? For the right to see if what she wanted to say would be taken in the spirit that she gave it? He knew that look, had seen it on his own face in the mirror as a child when his mother had warned him not to tell anyone about anything that went on inside their family.

'I once read the Bible backwards,' she began. 'It was after my mother left my father for a lover who killed her.' She looked up. 'Not physically, you understand. There are other ways for people to die.'

Other ways? Small ways and large. Hearts that broke bit by bit until there was nothing left of any of it. Confidences that squeezed the very life out of living!

'Her lover was a man like you…secretive, dark…' Her voice broke on the confession.

Lord. Just like him! And in so many more ways than she knew.

But she did not let it go. 'If my father hears that I have told you this…'

'He won't.' The hands at the side of her gown were balled into tight fists.

'You promise me?'

'On my very life,' he returned, an odd expression that Nat and Hawk and him had used as boys when trading secrets.

'I had not meant to say, it was only…' She stopped.

'Only that I had aired my skeletons in the cupboard and you felt obliged to do the same?

He was pleased when she smiled. 'Only that.'

Far away the shape of Woodruff Abbey stood against a dark line of trees, nestled in a wide and fertile valley. Figures played on the lawn and on the circular sweep of driveway.

'How long have you been the children's guardian?'

'Since I put Woodruff into trust for them and named myself a trustee.'

'The place is not yours?'

'It is mine to use, but theirs to keep.'

'An expensive gift from a man with little in the way of chattels.'

'Children need a safe home to grow up in.'

'A home like the one you never had. Whatever happened to your parents' house? You have not mentioned it at all.'

'It was sold when they left England. Travel is expensive and my father could never abide the responsibility of chattels.'

'He sounds a selfish man.'

When he didn't answer she tried another tack. 'The little girls seem very fond of you?'

This time when he laughed Lillian felt the warmth of it and she liked the sound, liked the easy way he tipped back his head, liked the creases that marked the skin around his eyes when he did so. Not a dandy or a fop. No, her husband was a man whom the outdoors had marked in muscle and in tone, the bronze in his eyes startling sometimes against the darkness of his skin. Like now, outlined against the wideness of sky, a man who could have been one of those wild Danish thanes wandering this part of the land all those centuries ago. That was it exactly. He did not really fit into England with its gentle rhythms and thin watery sun.

And he was hers. For a lifetime. This man whom she did not understand, but wanted to, this man whose body called to her own in a way no others ever had before him. She felt humbled by his confession of the Woodruff trust, humble enough to offer him money and condolences for his lack of property

'Fairley Manor is a large estate. You should want for nothing with my dowry.'

'I would never challenge your right to Fairley, Lilly. I swear it. If you wanted, I could have my lawyer draw up a document to say just that.'

Lillian was speechless at his sincerity. How often in her life had she been pursued by swains who measured the value of the Davenport lands before the worth of taking her as a bride? Yet here was a man with little who would give it all back?

'Fairley is your heritage and, just as Hope and Charity need a home, so do you.'

The understanding in his answer was exactly what she needed and the awareness between them heightened.

Touch me! she longed to ask. Reach out first and

touch me, for she could not do it, not after the words she had given him of squandering and patience and anger.

But he only swiped away a winged insect that dived down and laughed as she jumped back.

'It likes the light in your hair. How long is it when you wear it down?'

'My hair?' She blushed beetroot red. 'Too long, probably. I should cut it, but—'

'No.' A frown crossed his forehead, emotion skewered by his need for caution.

In answer she simply undid the net that held her chignon in place, enjoying the feel of curls unravelling down her back, the length reflected by the greed in his eyes.

'It was patience I asked for,' she whispered softly, 'not distance.'

'Ah, Lilly,' he replied in return, 'have caution with what you think a husband might take from such an offer.'

Still he did not move.

'Perhaps a little?' Her tongue licked around the sudden dryness of her lips.

'A little?' His voice was husky as he reached forwards and brought him to her, not gently either, but moulded along the full front of each other so that she felt the hard angles of his body and the heat of his breath.

'Is this a little?' he asked as his lips came down upon her own, opening her mouth and plundering, one hand sliding up from her waist to fist in her hair and the other cupping her chin as though daring her to pull away.

She didn't, the taste of him exactly how she had remembered it in countless dreams, an invitation for more, his tongue laving against hers, the rocking of his body restless and every breath shared.

Heady delight in the fold of an ancient mountain and the wind playing with her hair, the shards of need swelling want in her belly, in her breasts, in the place between her legs that no man had ever touched.

She could not feel where she ended and he began, could not in truth stop him from doing anything that he wanted, the brutal slam of lust as desperate in her as she could feel it was in him. Just pleasure, on the edge of delight, just the boneless floating relief of what it was to be a woman, and at twenty-five it had been a long time coming.

When he finally broke off the kiss she pressed in, but he held her still, his breathing ragged and his voice hoarse.

'The rain is near and a little is never enough.'

His heart beat in the same rhythm as hers, matching exactly as her hands bunched at the material in his jacket, trembling with what had just happened, no control and no regrets either, the core of her being alive with the rightness of it.

This had nothing to do with the expectation of others, for no external thing could touch a freeing blazing truth that held all the other more normal concerns at a distance.

What if she had not constrained him with 'a little', what if she had just let him do what it was he seemed so very good at, up here on the high mountain with no one around them for miles?

Always a limit, the boundaries of her life reflected even in her loving. The thought made her frown as she tied up her hair, feeling a little like a fairytale princess who had been let out of a story for just a moment.

Princess Lillian. How often had unkind children called her that as she had grown up? The girl with everything!

Except a mother, and the rigid morals of her father the touchstone to his affection.

She took in a deep breath and moved away, not meeting the gaze of her husband, though his smile she could not fail to miss even from the corner of her eyes.

'For a woman who has barely been kissed in her life you have made remarkable progress.'

Not a criticism, then. With her confidence bolstered she faced him. 'I have had a good teacher.'

'And one with a lot more to show you yet.'

His laughter caught on the wind and the cloak she wore billowed as if even her clothes sought closer contact, both the strength and mystery in him evident in the way he watched her, as if 'just a little' would never be enough.

Chapter Sixteen

Lucas was not at breakfast at all the next morning, a fact that Lillian found strange; by the middle of the afternoon she was beginning to wonder just exactly where hc was, for he had left in the early evening of the previous day and had been more than a little distracted. She had been glad when he had come to tell her of his need to leave Woodruff for a few hours because the kiss of the afternoon lingered still, clouding every reasonable argument she thought of that might stop her going further.

Her daydreams were vivid and passion-filled. No constraint on imagination after what had happened yesterday. Now her mind followed other paths, unbridled and giddy paths that had no mind for limits and no time for a marriage convened in name only.

The dress she wore today seemed to mirror all her thoughts, the lace trimming it barely covering places that she had always kept well shielded. She had put it on in hope that Lucas would be back to see it, but by midday had given up on that hope and had begun instead to explore Woodruff Abbey.

After a good half an hour she found a room off a conservatory at one end of the house containing a library whose shelves gave the impression of having never being culled since the first literate member of the family had begun to call the Abbey home. Sitting in a chair, she was looking at a book with various lithographs of Bath when she became aware of a rustling behind her, the quick order of quiet that came after it telling her that it was the children that she had met two nights back.

Hope and Charity.

Whilst wondering what mother in her right mind would saddle her children with such names, a small white winter rose hit her on the arm. And then another one.

Playing the game, she rose and picked them up, cradling them in her hand.

'Why, it is flower snow…'

The whispering stopped to be replaced by silence.

'Fairies send this to earth to remind children of their manners.' She looked around, making an effort not to glance in the direction of an old table that she knew them to be behind.

A small giggle could be heard.

'But this does not sound like a fairy laugh…?' She moved forwards meaning to take the game further, but Hope's face poked out before she could.

'It is us,' she said simply, like a child who did not have a great knowledge of how to play at make-believe and pretend. 'We picked the flowers from the garden yesterday before the rain,' she qualified, looking out of the windows that graced the whole wall of this wide room. Drops distorted the glass, the heavy greyness outside making everything colder within.

Charity came out from behind her, both children dressed in identical matching aprons.

'You have been doing your lessons?'

Hope's face contorted. 'We did not have to do anything until a month ago when Mr Lucas said that we must and he found us a tutor.'

'Learning is a good thing,' Lillian countered, gesturing to the book she held. 'Reading can give you many hours of happiness.'

The children did not answer, but looked at her with uncertain faces. Trying to find some topic that might be of more interest, she happened on the season.

'Do you make decorations with your governess?'

Both little girls shook their heads. 'Mrs Wilson tells us that we are too old for Christmas now.'

'Too old for Christmas?' Suddenly she felt unreasonably angry towards a woman who would tell two motherless little girls such a fib. 'No one is too old for Christmas. It is a fact.'

Hope crept closer. 'Last year we brought a tree in from outside. Mrs Poole let us thread paper to decorate it and she cooked lovely things like plum pudding. But this year it is different. We just have to study because Mrs Wilson tells us we have missed out on so much knowledge.'

Charity nodded behind her, giving Lillian the impression of hearing every word her sister said. So she was not deaf!

Different for Lillian, too, the bare lack of seasonal joy all around this room suddenly rankling. 'If I was able to find some paper and paint and scissors and glue, would you be able to help me decorate this room?'

'Now?'

'As it is only just over a week until Christmas we have no more time to waste.'

Charity's little head bobbed up and down, the first time Lillian had seen her decide something before her sister and for a second she opened her mouth as if she might speak, but she didn't, and with her blonde-white hair and pale eyes she suddenly reminded her of someone.

Herself as a young child! Trying to please. Apprehensive. Motherless. She swallowed back sadness, the great wave of grief catching her sideways. She had not cried when her mother had left because her father had needed strength and fortitude, and she had not cried after Rebecca's death either because by then the ingrained habit of coping had taken hold.

Coping!

How good once she had been at that.

'We have some silver ribbon and tiny pinecones in

boxes in our room, Lilly. Would that be useful, do you think?'

'Indeed it would be.' Lillian placed the book she had been browsing back on to its shelf and held out her arms to the girls. When two small warm hands crept into her own she had the sudden thought that she had never before touched a child or even been close to one. And when her own fingers curled into theirs she also realised just how much she had missed out on.

Luc returned just as dusk was falling on the land, the rain that had been present all day as a downpour becoming more like a shower, the drops of it caught in the last shards of light.

Woodruff stood in a rainbow, its lines etched against a leaden sky. Like a treasure, he thought to himself, at the end of a rainbow. Lilly and Charity and Hope.

He pushed the gun he held into the saddlebag and took his knife from where it was hidden in his sock, tucking it in beside the pistol. His sleeve he pulled down too, the deep cut on his forearm so obviously from a blade he wanted no one to see it.

Daniel Davenport had just sat down for a drink in a pub near Fairley when Lucas had surprised him, and the two other fellows drinking with him, who were familiar, their hands filled today with drink instead of the batons in London when they had waylaid him on the city streets.

Davenport had scampered quickly away and Luc

swore at the memory of it before looking up. The day was dark though it was barely evening and Christmas was close. Perhaps it was the seasonal tidings, then, that explained his leniency with the others' lives, discharging the pair into the hands of the local constabulary before making his way back to Woodruff. Even six weeks ago he would have had no compunction in killing them, but the influence of Lilly upon everything seemed to have trickled even into his need for revenge.

'Damn,' he muttered as a branch whipped across him, pain marking his face when it dug into his aching arm, where one of the pair had surprised him with a hidden knife. The lights of the house were bright and the sound of music came from within.

Christmas music, he determined as he got closer.

Sing choirs of angels
Sing in exaltation
Sing all ye citizens of Heaven above

The first pelt of a heavier rain made him grimace as he turned his horse for the stables and prepared to dismount.

They had worked all afternoon on the library, pulling an aged pianoforte from its covers to set it up near the tree Mr Poole had cut for them, which was now adorned haphazardly in red and green and gold and silver. Stars, hearts and twirling paper cut-outs bedecked each branch and plaited chains ran from an angel at the very top: an angel fashioned from an old doll of Hope's. A roaring fire burned now in the grate and chased the dark shadowed coldness from the room.

Festive and bright, the smell of sharp evergreen was in the air and the sound of crackling chestnuts on the hotplate above the flames.

Not a white or a pale shade on show. Lillian thought of her perfectly decorated rooms at Fairley, so different from this, the expensive trimmings laid in exactly the same pattern each and every year.

Yet here with the children's governess on the pianoforte, Mrs Poole singing her heart out beside her and the children in their night attire snuggled in, Lillian felt a certain peace of spirit that she had never known before. She had never sung the carols like this at the top of her voice with no care for tune or melody, had never eaten her supper on a tray with mismatched utensils and a flower across the top of the plate that looked as if it had been in a storm for weeks. But Charity had picked it from the garden between the showers and handed it to her shyly, so Lillian had given it pride of place, the lurid blood-red reminiscent of Lucas's taste in blooms. Hope traced the shape of her wedding ring as the song came to an end, one of the cats trying to lick the icing sugar from her fingers.

'I do not like your ring much, Lilly. When I get married I shall have a slender band with one single diamond.'

Lillian laughed, the truth of it so naïvely and honestly given, and at that moment Lucas stepped into the room.

* * *

She was laughing, the children beside her in a library that was completely changed. Things hung everywhere, Christmas things, all hand-fashioned, he surmised, and a tree stood where before had been only a chair.

His library. Gone. Replaced by a grotto of light and sound, hot chocolate drinks on the tables and a pianoforte that he had not known was there.

His arm ached and the faces of those he had tracked today danced macabrely before him.

Juxtaposition.

His life had always been full of it. But here tonight it was a creeping reminder of wrongness, a shout from the empty spaces he inhabited and people who made the world a place unsafe.

He tried to smile, tried to feel the warmth, tried to know all that it was he knew he missed, his sodden clothes making him shiver unexpectedly.

'Lucas.' Lilly's voice was soft and the children acknowledged him from her lap.

'I am wet. If you would give me a moment to change.'

He turned before anyone could say otherwise because shaking began to claim him, deep and strong, the blood loss from his arm, he suspected, combined with the extreme cold on a long ride home. 'I will be back soon…' he called the words over his shoulder and when the music began to play again he was pleased.

Glory to God
In the Highest
Oh, come let us adore him…

Something was not right, she could tell it in his laboured gait and in the sound of his words. A hidden sound that she knew well, her own voice having the same timbre in it for all those years.

'No, I am all right, Father, I will be down soon.'

If only her father had not believed her. If only he had come in to her room and held her warm against the demons and the regrets and the guilt of everything that had happened with her mother. But he had not and she had got better and better at hiding what she wanted others not to see. Like Lucas tonight!

Settling the children on the pillows and excusing herself, she walked up the stairs to the second floor.

The door to his room was shut, a room she had discovered today on their search for materials to use for the decorations and she could hear nothing inside.

Deciding against knocking, she turned the handle and stepped in.

He lay on his bed fully dressed, one hand across his face, the wetness of the night staining the counterpane dark and he shivered violently.

'I will be down soon, Lillian.' He did not remove his hand, did not try to rise or sit or converse further. The skin she could see around his lips was blue.

Fright coursed through her. 'You are ill?'

'No, I am c-cold. If you could just leave…'

One golden eye became visible through the slit of his fingers when she did not go. 'If you could hand me the b-blankets?' Tiredness ringed his eyes, a crippling desperate tiredness that did not just come from lack of sleep, his speech slurred into a stutter. She noticed how his left arm lay limp by his side, the deeper stain of blood showing at his wrist.

Blood! Hurrying over, she took his fingers into her own. Freezing.

'I will call a doctor.'

He shook his head and dry terror coated Lilly's mouth. Not a simple accident, then, if he thought to hide it! Carefully she rolled back the sleeve and the long thin jagged wound took away her breath.

'Who has done this?

Silence reigned and she had the impression that he was holding in his breath until he could cope with the pain. 'It was my own fault,' he finally said and she knew she would hear no more.

'It looks deep.'

'Are you very good at s-stitching?'

'Tapestries. Embroideries. I can sew up the hem of a gown if I have to…' Suddenly she saw where this was going and her voice petered out.

The side of his lips curled up. 'I am certain then that th-this will give you no b-bother. But it will n-need to be cleaned first.'

'With what?' Lillian felt her teeth clench in worry.

She had had no practice of this sort of thing ever. Oh, granted, she had dealt with headaches before and the occasional bruise, but a conserve of red roses and rotten apple in equal parts wrapped in thin cambric did not quite seem the answer here.

'Alcohol. The more proof the better, and boiling water. If you fetch Mrs Poole, she will know what to do.'

Lillian suddenly felt sick to her stomach. 'This has happened before?'

He turned away from her criticism, a man only just dealing with the agony of his arm and not up to telling any more of the truth. She jumped up in fright when his eyes turned back in his head and all that was left was the white in them. Quickly he shook himself and burning amber reappeared.

'If you die, Lucas Clairmont, two days after I have married you, I swear that I will strangle you myself.'

Her words were no longer careful, the shout in them surprising them both.

It made no sense, but she was beyond caring, beyond even the measuring of right and wrong. If he had killed someone today, then the reckoning of his soul would come to him later. Right now she just had to get him better.

With the room warmed by a blazing fire and his sodden shirt removed, Lucas's shivering finally stopped.

Mrs Poole brought steaming water and sharp scissors and all her movements gave the impression of a woman who had seen such things before.

'I was with Wellington's troops, my dear,' she explained when Lillian asked her. 'Marched with the drum, you see. It was how I met Mr Poole, for my first husband had been killed in Spain and widows did not stay that way for long.'

'And you saw injuries such as this one?'

'Many a time.'

'And they lived…' she whispered, 'those who had this sort of injury?'

'Of course they did. It's only if they took the fever after I would worry, though it is a pity he will not allow himself a good swig of brandy, for the ache would be a lot lessened.'

She handed a needle and thread to Lillian. 'Take little stitches and not too deep. Are you certain you would not like some brandy, my dear?'

Having already refused libation once, Lillian shook her head. She needed to be completely in control for the task in front of her and wished for the twentieth time that Mrs Poole's eyesight had been better.

Still, with the long explanation as to what the housekeeper could and could not see behind them, Lillian thought it only right that it should be her doing the repair work.

'I've had stitches before,' Lucas said to her as she readied herself for the task, trying to put it off for as long as she could. 'I don't usually weep.'

The tilt of his lips told her that he was attempting to take some of the tension from the moment, though the sweat on his upper lip gave a different story again. Not quite as indifferent as he would have her think! Her heart beat so violently she could visibly see the rise and fall of her bodice and it accelerated markedly again as she learnt that skin was a lot harder than cloth to push a needle through.

'I'm so sorry,' she whispered as he winced, the quick spring of red blood from the wound blotted by Mrs Poole as he looked away. Following his glance, she saw that the night outside was still heavy with rain and further afield the bright glow of lightning silhouetted the land.

'A storm is coming this way,' he said and Mrs Poole interjected.

'There is talk of snow, sir. Perhaps it will be a white Christmas after all.'

The weather was a benign topic as the needle sliced through flesh again and again, the stitches neat and tidy and his skin once jagged and open pulled together into a single light red line.

When it was done, Lillian put down her needle and stood, the magnitude of all that had happened washing over her in a flood of shock.

'Thank you.' In the soft light of flame his amber eyes were grateful, bleached in fatigue and something else, too.

Embarrassment.

When Mrs Poole bustled out of the room in search of a salve that was missing, Lillian also felt…shy. Wiping her hands against her skirt, the enormity of everything overcame her.

'If you are in trouble, perhaps I can help. My father has money and influence. If I talked to him and asked—'

'No, Lillian.' He winced as he shifted his position on the bed, the pale hue of his face alarming her.

His use of the fullness of her name surprised her as did the tone he used, as serious as she had ever heard him, his accent almost English.

'When I left you in the Billinghurst ballroom in London, I walked into a trap.'

'A trap?' She could not understand at all what he was telling her.

'Three men jumped me as I made my way home from the ball and the next thing I knew I was on a ship as a prisoner heading for Lisbon. I think Davenport money was used to make me…disappear.'

Lillian put her hand across her mouth to try to stop the horror that was building. 'I would never…'

'Not you.' His smile was gentle, relief showing over tenderness.

'My father?' The horror of his confession was just beginning to be felt. Lord, if it were her father…

'Not him either.'

'Daniel, then?'

'And his mother. A woman paid the money and the Davenport coach was waiting at the end of the alley.'

'Aunt Jean?' Horror tripped over her question. 'I cannot believe that my aunt would pay for something so… wrong.'

A flicker of a smile crossed his face, though there was

something he was not telling her, something that marked his eyes with carefulness even as he stayed silent.

'When you did not come back, I thought perhaps you were in hiding, not wanting to be betrothed by force to me.'

He shook his head. 'I had my lawyer offer marriage as soon as I heard of…of how things were for you.' Lillian was glad he did not say ruined.

'And when my father accepted, I could never understand just how it was you persuaded him.'

A shutter fell across amber, the secrets between them there again after a few brief moments of honesty. The thought made her sad as she tidied the sheets on his bed.

'There are things we need to say to each other, Lilly, but not here like this. I need to at least be standing.' The corners of his lips pulled up.

'An explanation for your wounds, perhaps?' She gestured to his arm and unexpectedly he reached out, the strength in his fingers belying the pain.

'That, too,' he added and the brush of his thumb traced the lines of blueness on her wrist. A small caress! Quietly given as the distant storm rolled closer and a single bolt of lightning lit the room with yellow, thunder rattling the panes of glass in a celestial reminder of the paltriness of human construction and endeavour.

When his fingers tightened she did not pull away, liking the warmth and closeness, watching the wind wild-tangled in the trees outside.

He was asleep before she realised it, his face in slumber so different from the watchful guardedness that cloaked him when awake. The scar on his neck was easily seen, his head tipped sideways so that the full length of it was visible, his opened collar making it even more shocking.

A small boy who had left parentless for the new lands across the sea. What had happened to him between then and now? she wondered. What possible excuse could he give for the scraps he was so constantly in?

'Please, God, don't let him be…bad,' she asked quietly of the omnipotent deity that she believed in, and then smiled at her own ridiculous description of Lucas's character.

Bad?

From whose point of view?

The world she lived in skewered slightly. Never before had she questioned anything. Rules. Regulations. Beliefs. All had been adhered to in the way of one who feared that even the slightest of detours might lead to chaos.

Well it had, here and now, but the feel of his fingers against hers and the sound of his breathing did not feel like anarchy.

No, it felt warm and real and right, the world held at bay by a promise far greater than fear.

'Love,' she said quietly into the darkness, the word winding around truth with its own particular freedom as Mrs Poole bustled back with a tray full of salves.

Chapter Seventeen

Lucas joined them for breakfast, the morning weather quieter than it had been in the night. Today, Lillian could almost feel the sun wanting to break through its binding mantle of cloud, though a thick blanket of twigs and leaves had been left on the part of the garden visible from the breakfast room.

Hope chattered beside her about the day and the night and the storm and the decorations that they had made yesterday. A never-ending array of topics and thoughts and so different from her sister, who sat in silence as she carefully spooned thick porridge to her lips.

'If your governess could spare you one day around lunchtime, I thought we could go and collect pine cones and berries for the Christmas fireplace. I used to do the same when I was a little girl.'

'At Fairley?' Luc asked.

She nodded. 'With my mother…' Amazement claimed

her. She could not remember the last time she had ever spoken of her mother in company, but as the questioning gazes of the two children fell upon her she fought to appear calm. 'She died when I was thirteen and I find it sad to think of her. Especially at Christmas.'

Unexpectedly Charity's warm hand crept into hers, the small honesty of it endearing. *You are not alone*, it said. *I'm here.*

Lillian looked at Luc, knowing that he had seen the gesture, and he tipped his head. This morning the whiteness of his shirt covered the generous bandage and his colour had returned to normal. A masculine virile man with more than just humour in his smile, for sensuality and appetite could be seen there, too. She knew by the responding lurch of her own body that it would not be long before pure desire ruled between them.

Looking away, she helped herself to scrambled egg and a piece of thick buttered toast. Scrambled like her thoughts, the rush of heat on her cheeks bringing her glance downwards so that her new husband might not see, might not know, might not understand that the resistance she had made such a show of was crumbling fast.

'I have something in my room for you, Lilly. When you have finished your breakfast and the girls have gone up to their lessons I would like to give it to you.'

His room was tidier than she had seen it last time, all the clothes put away and the myriad of papers and books stacked on his desk into two neat piles.

A well-read man, she determined, and tried to align that with one who gambled and fought. Often.

She noticed there were many books on boats and shipping and on a shelf behind him was a single ship on a plinth, its riggings intricate and complete.

'She's the *Rainbow*,' he said when he saw her looking, 'and one of the prettiest clippers ever built by Donald McKay. I saw her once in Massachusetts Bay before she made for the open sea with her long fine bow. She was designed to penetrate through the waves, you see, rather than ride over them.'

'You bought this model here?'

He nodded. 'In London. It will be shipped home to my uncle's house in Richmond after Christmas.'

'He likes ships as well?'

'Liked. He is dead.'

'Did your parents ever visit you in America?'

'No, thank God.' When she frowned, he softened the criticism. 'My parents were more interested in each other than in me. My father was almost forty when I was born and heavy-handed with a boy whom they never understood. It was a relief when they left my upbringing to Stuart.'

'But you saw them again after you left England?'

He shook his head. 'They died a few years after I left, of the influenza. In Italy.'

She saw no sorrow in his eyes. Just fact and distance, the ties that more usually held a boy to his parents broken by misunderstanding.

'So you lived with your uncle.'

When he hesitated she knew that he had not. 'I lived on his land on the James and farmed it.'

'By yourself?'

'There were a few mishaps but I soon got the way of it and Stuart helped me.'

'Did one of the mishaps lead to the scarring on your neck?'

Before he could stop himself he pulled up his collar, the movement making Lillian place her hand upon his arm. 'It was not meant as a censure,' she said softly.

'I have other scars as well,' he returned and the air around them changed.

Other scars, other places. Where she could not see? Beneath his clothes and hidden. A singular vision of naked limbs entwined came to her, the thick burgundy cover on his bed loosely wrapped around them.

'I am not untarnished, Lillian,' he went on. 'Not like you,' he added, the husky American accent in his voice more pronounced than she had ever heard it. 'And I cannot help but notice that you rarely wear my ring.'

He brought her hand up between them, the nakedness of her finger making her frown.

'I took it off yesterday when I was painting with the girls…'

He leaned over and opened the drawer by his bed. 'I know. Mrs Poole found it and had it cleaned.' The large red ruby glinted at her, its familiar heaviness making it less…ugly, she thought, surprising herself. When he fitted it on to her finger she smiled.

In return he traced a line from her wrist to her elbow and then higher again when she did not pull away or turn.

'I want this marriage to be more than just a sham, more than separate beds. You mentioned patience and limitations, but I am thinking that I have run out of both.'

'I see.' Her answer was given with a smile.

'So if you thought to stop me, then I would say now is about the time…'

His fingers cupped the fullness of one breast through the layer of velvet, his burning glance holding her captive.

The feeling was exquisite. Thin want with need on the edge of it, and an answering spasm in her belly as the thrall of lust made her groan out aloud.

'Lucas?'

She whispered his name amongst the riding waves of hunger and heat, his leg pushing against the mound of her femininity.

'I would like to show you more than just a kiss under mistletoe, Lilly.'

His breath against her face was close. A locked door and as many hours as was needed.

She felt his fingers move across the cloth of her gown, bringing her to him. The length of their bodies fused into warmness, finding home, fitting perfectly.

When she tipped up her head he leant down, his mouth tasting hers, slanting across the small kiss she thought to offer and finding much, much more.

Heat. Hope. Thrall.

The pulse in her quickened, understanding what she knew only such a little of, yet wanting again what he had offered her once, the strength and core of his masculinity measured and fine.

And then hesitating.

'Why?' She shook her head, her breathing hoarse in the silence and the daylight bright. Not dark. Not hidden. No concealed and veiled mating.

'If we go any further, Lillian, I cannot promise to cease.'

'Cease?' Even the thought of it made her shake.

'It is not just a kiss I want this time.'

She felt her face flame, though his answering smile was tender.

'I would never mean to hurt you.'

'Hurt me?' Her eyes widened, reality coming between fantasy.

She heard him take in breath and hold it. His heartbeat quickened under the pads of her fingers at his wrist.

'When a man and a woman mate, the way of it is not always easy the first time.'

His words were whispered, the clock on his desk punctuating the passing seconds of silence. The caress of his breath on her cheeks made her turn towards him even as he began to speak again.

'Do you know anything of what happens?'

Lillian swallowed. 'A baby is made by the seed you place in my stomach.' Anne Weatherby had told her that once after a particularly large glass of wine.

'Well, not quite, sweetheart.'

Sweetheart? The word turned in her mind. Not a small endearment from a man who looked as he did.

Lucas's hands had now fallen lower, caressing her hips and her stomach and an ache of want made her press into him, unbidden. Asking for more even without the knowledge of what 'more' meant.

He began to move too, matching her rocking with his own. Give and take! The silent language of lovers through all the centuries of time. Faster and harder until her fingernails scraped down the skin of his arms, trying to understand what it was she asking for. Just this. Just them.

'Luc?' A question almost groaned. His fingers cupped her chin and he brought her face up so that his amber eyes burnt into hers as his other hand fell lower.

And lower as he lifted her skirt. The coolness of the winter air was strange against the heat of his fingers, and when he reached into what was hidden she tried to look away. He did not let her, holding his glance to her own as one finger gently found what it sought and eased in.

The rush of delight was elemental, uncomplicated and right. Opening her legs further, a thicker push followed, his fingers magic in what they engendered, a play of feeling and need and rapture.

The rising hardness against her stomach made her wonder. Was a man's need as great as hers, but nowhere near as well concealed? She smiled at the thought.

'Like a sheath, Lilly,' he said as he nuzzled her neck. 'I promise that you will fit me like a sheath.'

Snug? Close? Bound in skin?

Again he took her mouth, using his tongue in the same way he did his fingers, penetrating to find knowledge of her. Time seemed to stop as the day faded into only feeling, a nip of his teeth against the soft skin of her lips, his other hand pushing away the fabric covering her breasts and cupping the fullness before finding her nipple. And below his fingers bathed now in wetness.

The air between them quivered with all that he was doing to her, sweat building across the skin of her body as waves of need seemed to grow and grow and then recede again as he pulled away.

'No!' He laughed at her fervency, though his voice seemed hoarse and different.

'Not so fast. Not so fast.'

Peeling away her stockings, he settled her against the wall, her velvet gown a cushion against the cold and her skirt now riding high above the juncture of her legs. Naked. Bare. Waiting. Excitement built steadily, vying with impatience as he undid his trousers and slid them down. The billowing white of his cotton shirt contrasted against the brown of his skin, muscles firmed and well defined.

A beautiful man with golden eyes and night-black hair and enough experience to make all of this easy! Giddy delirium urged her on, her fingers coming to the abundance of his sex and feeling…him. Smooth, warm. Needing all of what was to happen next. No control. No limitations. Just all the hours before them and an aching yearning eagerness!

He brought her hand into his as he positioned himself

at the juncture of her legs. Wetness flooded between them and she frowned.

'It is your body, sweetheart, saying that you want me.'

Now he lifted her slightly, gently piercing.

'Luc,' she cried as the first pains hit, his length buried within and straining.

He stopped instantly, his breath ragged and his eyes pleading.

'If you truly wish for me to cease…'

'No.' She whispered this time, for in the hurt she could detect some other want, a small question of flesh as he moved once and once again.

Bringing her legs around him, he tipped her hips and her weight upon his manhood changed from discomfort into another thing.

Some life-filled thing, her hands holding him in place as her mouth bit into the soft folds of his neck.

Not just her hurt, but his as well, the deep thrusts changing rhythm, harder and faster, careful wariness punctured by a building fervour as his hand covered her bottom. The crescendo of an ache made her throw her head back and just feel, the pulse of heat and light and loving. And sound. Her voice. Not restrained or polite or ladylike, but vivid and raw and loud.

Nothing hidden or covert! No shrouded thing as the pace of their breathing slowed and the world reformed again.

'This is what all married people feel…?' She had to ask.

'Only those who are lucky enough,' he returned and

lifted her into his arms, the swell of her breasts displaced so that her nipples were easily on show.

When he laid her on his bed she sat there as he undid her gown and her stays, pulling the cloth from her nakedness, daylight revealing much more than just secrets.

'My God, you are so very beautiful,' he said slowly, unravelling her hair. 'Far more beautiful out of your clothes than in them and that's saying something.' The heavy drop of her tresses reached to the small of her back and the warmth was welcome.

Lucas wrapped his fingers in the gold paleness and brought it up to the light.

'So many different shades of pale, Lilly.' He had never seen hair her colour on anybody before, a changing kaleidoscope of corn and wheat and silver, her skin mirroring the delicate fineness. Carefully he shrugged off his shirt and stepped from his trousers, though when the bandage on his arm chaffed against his side he saw her wonder, all the other scars he had kept hidden beneath clothes visible as well today in the morning light.

Lillian's fingers traced the one on his thigh and then the smaller scar beneath his left rib. 'A bullet where I was not quick enough,' he said when he saw where it was she looked.

Her body glowed in unmarked glory, the long lines of her legs, the roundness of her bottom and the smooth beauty of her breasts. Only one finger held the slice of some accident. He found the hand and separated it from the others.

'I hurt it on a knife last year when I was quartering the first apple of summer.'

He laughed. Even her accidents were appealing. The ruby ring on her finger winked at him as he turned her hand.

'Do you still want this changed?'

She shook her head.

'I have grown used to it and it has grown used to me.'

'It was my grandmother's and the only possession I took with me from England. I wore it on a chain then around my neck so that it would not be stolen when I worked my passage. I never gave it to my first wife and now I know why. I was waiting for you.'

Her hand fisted tight and he leant to place a kiss on the back of her knuckles, laving the spaces between with his tongue, the trail of coldness making Lillian shiver.

Her husband. A man fashioned by hardship and loneliness and the absence of family that had shaped all of his life.

And now. What was he now? Just at this moment in this room with their skin against the daylight and the feel of each so known?

Lovers? Friends? Two halves of a whole made complete? The beginning of a life that glinted in the red stone on her finger, tantalisingly close.

'Love me, Lucas,' she whispered.

'I do,' he answered and his mouth came down to claim hers in reply.

* * *

He had left when she woke, the dent in the sheets where he had lain, cold and empty.

Her hand smoothed down the creases and she turned towards his side so that she lay watching the window, the smile that played at her lips pushing into the pillow with a shy incredulity.

'Goodness,' she whispered, remembering. She had always been so controlled, so restrained, so correct and careful and proper.

But not this morning!! The hours with Luc had cured her of ever being *proper* again, his hands in places she had not dreamed of, and showing her things she could never have imagined. Stretching, she felt elation rise. She was a wife in truth now, and one who knew the secrets of a marriage bed.

A tiny piece of misdoubt remained as she also thought of the marks that crossed his body. No little accidents or paltry cuts. The scar on his leg ran from his groin to his knee and the one at his neck reached the blade of his shoulder. And that was discounting the long wound still beneath the bandage. She frowned. The man who had left England as a boy had had enemies; that much was certain. Still had enemies, she corrected.

Could she ask him about it? Would he tell her? Her father had seldom spoken to her mother of anything of importance. She knew because Rebecca had complained of it again and again to her friends when she thought Lillian was not listening.

Was this the way of marriage? She shook her head and played with her ring. In the light the stone shone red against the sheets, and in the newly cleaned yellow gold she saw markings. Slipping the bauble off, she brought it up to her eyes and read an inscription of three words held within the band.

Whither thou goest...

Lillian finished it off from memory in a whisper. '...I will go: and where thou lodgest I will lodge.'

She sat up, the declaration of devotion from the Book of Ruth making her heart thump. Did Lucas know these letters lay within the ring? Had he meant them for her? The band was an old one, fashioned, she imagined, some time in the last century, the worth of it considerable. Had it been only recently engraved or was it an ancient troth given between other lovers? His grandmother's, he had said, and the only worldly tie to a family lost to him. Slipping it back on, she clenched her hand inwards, the value of gold and precious stone as nothing compared to the worth of the words.

A shimmer of hope crossed her heart like a kiss beneath the magic of mistletoe or the first dusting of fine snow when the Christmas bells rang true.

New! Exciting! Full of promise!

Pushing back the sheets, she stood, donning a nightgown left on the oak chest at the foot of his bed, the material holding the smell of Lucas and the folds of fabric easily reaching to her feet. With care she pulled the bedding upwards so that the prying eyes of the maids she summoned would not see the chaos that such loving had wreaked and then she waited for a hot bath to be filled.

There were two men in the library with her husband when she went to find him a few hours later. Two men who looked nothing like refined country folk or city gentlemen.

Dangerous.

The word came out of nowhere and made her stop, fright replacing all that had been there a moment earlier, and Lucas's expression daunted her further.

'Lillian.' His tone was distant but polite as he moved in front of the visitors, shielding them from her gaze. 'I am busy now. If you could wait until later?'

'Indeed?' She could not keep the question from her response, though nothing showed on his face save guardedness.

Looking further on to the desk, she noticed a pile of paper bank notes of the larger denominations and beside them lay a gun. Not the elegant shape of a duelling pistol, either, but the serious contours of a lethal shooting tool. The small Christmas tree that Charity had made him as a present sat squarely beside it, its red and silver stars the reminder of a season of goodwill and peace.

Not here though!

Not in this room!

Not with men who looked like foreign sailors or thieves, their eyes falling away from her own even as she glanced at them. Her right hand crossed her left, feeling for her ring.

'I will await you in the blue salon,' she added frostily, accepting her husband's help with the door as she sailed through it, the wide sway of her gown breaking the growing silence with its own particular music.

Once outside she stopped and took stock. Lucas's arm was out of the sling Mrs Poole had fashioned for him, and the clothes he wore were riding ones. Could he have been out already?

Eight days until Christmas and her house was filling up with guns, blood money and ruffians of a foreign persuasion, not to mention the chilling anger that had dwelt in her husband's eyes before he had been able to hide it.

She took three deep breaths and heard the sound of a squeal from the stairs.

Rounding the corner, she saw Hope and Charity playing with a puppy who looked nothing like any other dog she had ever seen. And Hope was calling to it, as it leapt to try to take a ball.

Lillian walked forwards. 'Where did the puppy come from, poppet?'

'Mrs Poole brought it over early this morning and Mr Lucas said we could keep it because Royce is getting to be so old. Can we, Lilly?' This entreaty, given her husband's promise already made, was so unexpected that she could not help but nod. Charity's head was bobbing up and down, too, and Lillian thought for a second that the child might even speak, for she pursed her lips in the way of a 'please'.

This morning could not possibly become any stranger, she thought. A husband sequestered with men who looked like pirates and a puppy dog with baby fat showing through the ample folds of its pink-and-white skin.

But when Stephen Hawkhurst suddenly burst through the front door in full riding kit and without knocking, she revised her opinion.

It just had!

Chapter Eighteen

'I need to speak to Lucas!' he shouted, the anger in his words causing the children and the puppy to cower behind her.

Her glance took in the sword in his scabbard and the holster containing a gun.

'Why, what on earth could be wrong—?' she began.

'Lillian, I have been lodging at the inn in the village in case of trouble. Tell me where Luc is, for the others are right behind me and there are many of them.' The anguish in his tone was unmistakable though his words petered out as her husband strode into the room.

'What the hell is happening?'

Stephen's eyes widened with relief. 'They are here, Luc.'

'You've seen them?'

'From the hill beyond the village! A group of six men coming this way. They will be here within a few minutes.'

Crossing the salon in three strides, Luc pulled her and the children towards the stairwell, depositing the frantic puppy into Hope's arms.

'Go up to our bedroom, Lilly, and lock the door. There is a gun in the drawer. Do you know how to use a gun?'

She shook her head.

'Then pretend you do,' he answered back, not phased at all by her ignorance. 'If anyone comes into the room, point it at their chest and buy some time.'

'Time,' she parroted, the whole idea of what it was he wanted beginning to make her shake, but already he had turned away and the men she had seen in the library were priming their own weapons.

'Come on, girls,' she said in a tone that she prayed was reassuring. 'We have many more Christmas decorations to make.'

When she saw her husband smile at her, the warmth in her heart warred with the whole terrible possibility that she, Lillian Davenport, had married a murderous and unrepentant stranger whose very soul was in utter and mortal danger.

Lucas took a breath as he watched his wife leave, her ridiculous comment about making Christmas decorations wringing a kind of respectful disbelief in him, the power of a woman's ability to shield children from anything dangerous so intrinsic in feminine virtue.

Virtue!

When had virtue deserted his life? At fourteen, perhaps, when he had worked out a hard passage to

America and learned things no youth should ever know. At twenty when the land he was breaking in demanded the sweat of a man twice his size and when the bank had no time for an injury that had nearly killed him? Or when Elizabeth had died in the mad dash to the midwife in Hampton while in labour with Daniel Davenport's child?

Consulting his uncle's watch, he checked the time. Something prosaic about that, too, he thought as he did it, given that Stuart Clairmont had long since run out of the same commodity.

The stealth of vengeance stilled him and he flipped a coin.

'Heads I get the gateway.'

Stephen smiled. 'Tails, you have the front door.'

When the florin showed the face of Victoria, Luc pushed open the portal and ran for it. He breathed in when no gunshots were heard, relief overcoming everything as his fingers tightened on the stock of the gun.

The beat of his heart and the sound of his breathing in the damp closeness of the day were all he could hear, save the wind in the trees on the far side of the gardens as he made his way around the pathway. The orange rosehips of the winter roses hung from their brown branch. If he came out of this he would pick them on his return and take them up to his wife. And then he promised himself he would tell her exactly who he was.

Lillian set the little girls the task of making a list of Christmas games that they would dearly like to play. She had instructed Hope to write out the rules so that they knew exactly how each game went and for Charity to make an illustration of it.

'Will Mr Lucas be all right, Lilly?' Charity's voice? Perfectly formed words with a voice that was slightly husky.

Lilly dropped to her knees in front of the child, tears behind her amazement. 'You can speak, Charity?'

'Oh, she always could, to me.' Hope was dismissive of such a momentous occasion. 'But she loves you, too, and so she chose to speak. When our mother died she just stopped, but with you here just like our mama…'

Lilly's hand went out to the little girl's face, brushing her fingers against one pale soft cheek.

'Thank you, Charity. Will you speak to Mr Lucas, too?' A shy little nod confirmed that she would and Lillian took her into her arms. As a mother would cuddle a child. Her child. Her children. Lucas and her and Hope and Charity. When the little girl broke away after a moment and returned to her drawings, Lilly moved across to Lucas's desk, surreptitiously wiping away her tears of gladness.

His drawer was full of pens and pencils and to one side she recognised the red-wax stamp of the Davenport family on a letter.

Why would he have that? She did not dare to unfurl the seal in case she could not rejoin it, but she could see Daniel's writing on the outside. Placing the letter down, she dug deeper into the drawer and brought out a set of

soldier's medals carelessly tangled and engraved with
the name of Lieutenant Lucas Clairmont from the 5th
Regiment of Infantry of the New York Militia. A date
stood out. 1844. Counting backwards, she determined
that would have made him all of twenty-four when he
had received them.

To one side of his desk on a sheet of paper she saw
her cousin Daniel's name scratched out beneath another.
Elizabeth Clairmont, Lucas's first wife. Had they known
each other in America? Could this be the reason for their
feud and for the letter here with the Davenport seal?

Lord! She could barely understand any of it.

Had she made love to a man who would tell her
nothing of the truth of his life, his whispers of something different more questionable now as she wondered
if she was a part of the same charade? No. She would
not think like that. She would not talk herself into the
wronged woman until she had spoken with her husband
and given him at least the chance to explain it all. When
the shouts of anger from beneath the window drifted
upwards she told Hope and Charity to stay down on the
floor and peeked most carefully out from the very
corner of the window.

To see a man take a shot at Lucas from the closest
of distances!

'Damn it,' Luc swore as the bullet mercifully missed
his head by the breadth of a farthing on its edge. 'You
should have taken a body shot,' the soldier in him

chided, though the man opposite was already re-cocking his pistol and he had no more time to lose.

His own bullet went true as the large man fell and a voice sounded out across the distance of the drive.

'If you don't come out now, I will shoot your friend.'

Daniel Davenport's voice, and then Stephen's!

'Don't do it, Luc. He will shoot me anyway—'

Hawk's voice was suddenly cut off. Not a shot, though. He had not heard that. The butt of a gun or the sharper bite of a sword? For Stephen's sake he prayed for the former.

Doubling back around the house, he had a good view of Davenport standing over Stephen and was pleased to see Lillian's cousin had absolutely no notion of him being there.

'Ten seconds or he dies. Nine…eight…seven….'

On the count of six Luc fired, the man to the left of Davenport falling without a fight.

'Damn,' he muttered, re-sighting his pistol and seeking the protection of the thick bough of a yew tree.

How many more men had Davenport brought and was Stephen still alive?

Looking around for anything he could use to his advantage, he found it in the heavy swathe of a hawthorn bush less than twenty yards away. If he could reach it, the plant would allow him an excellent cover to see around the whole side of the building.

Lillian saw Lucas meant to make a run for it, meant to leave his shelter and make for a spot further out and one that would allow him to see exactly where Lord Hawkhurst was. Goodness, if he should try she knew that he would never make it, the guns of those who held Hawkhurst firing before he would get there. If that happened they would be up the steps to the house next and she had very little wherewithal with which to protect the girls.

Could she open the window further and chance shouting out their positions? What if she threw something out to distract the men, to draw their fire this way whilst Lucas ran? The small solid wooden table next to her, for instance. She measured the width of the glass and, surmising it to fit, ordered Hope and Charity behind the sofa on the other side of the room.

Then she threw the piece of furniture with all her might, simply heaving it towards the middle of the glass and letting it go.

The shots came almost instantly, a wide round of them right at the window, pinging off its frame though one veered from the trajectory.

She felt it as a pinch, a tiny niggling ache that blossomed into a larger one, the red circle small at first and then spreading on the white of her dress. Breathing out, she sat down, her legs giving way to a dizzy swirling unbalance.

She heard the girl's screams through the numbing coldness and tried to take their hands, tried to reassure them, tried to tell them to stay down behind the sofa and out of harm's way.

But she couldn't because the dark and deepening blackness was leaching light from her world.

And then she knew nothing.

Luc was running, guns blazing past the hawthorn and around the corner, two men falling as he turned and another backing away.

Daniel Davenport. Today he looked nothing like the man from the drawing rooms of London and certainly nothing like the English lord who had held Elizabeth under his spell. No, today the fear in his eyes was all encompassing as the gun he cocked at Luc clicked empty.

His wife's lover.

Stuart's tormentor.

Retribution.

Pull the trigger and that would be the end of it. But he couldn't. Not in cold blood. Not with a man who looked him straight in the eyes.

'Kill him.' Stephen's words from the ground were said through pain and anger.

Lucas shook his head as Davenport spat at him, egging on a different and easier ending. But Luc merely smiled.

'Ruination to a man like this can be worse than death. When Society hears of your assault on my family home, you will never be welcomed in it again.'

The redness of Lillian's cousin's pallor faded to white, but Luc had more pressing matters to attend to. Giving the gun to Stephen and the gathering Woodruff servants he told them to lock Daniel up in the storeroom before he ran for the house and for Lilly, with every breath he took, praying she had not been hit by a stray bullet, though the girls' screams suggested otherwise.

'Lilly?' Her name called from a distance, a tunnel of blurred colour and a face close.

"Lilly.' He tried again and this time Lucas stood above her, dressed in the clothes he had been wearing when she…fell asleep? That wasn't right. It was night-time, and her curtains were shut, a lamp throwing the room into shadow.

'Thirsty.' She could barely croak out the word and when water was brought to her lips she tried to take big sips, but he drew it back.

'The doctor said just a little water and often.' Putting the glass on the table, he stepped back.

'Girls?'

'Are asleep after I promised them they could come to see you in the morning. Charity is chattering now even more than Hope. She sent you "a thousand kisses."'

'And Lord Hawkhurst?'

'Stephen is in the room next door with a bandaged head and two missing teeth.'

She nodded, the hugeness of all that had happened too great to contemplate right now. Lucas did not touch her, did not take her hand, did not sit on the empty chair beside the bed or fluff up her pillows. He looked angry, distracted and worried all at the same time.

Swallowing, the dryness in her mouth abated slightly

from the liquid, but she did not even want to know what had happened to her until she could cope.

Closing her eyes, she slept.

He was still there the next time she awoke. He slumbered on a chair, one leg balanced on a leather stool with a picture of an elephant engraved into it. His hands were crossed over his midriff, his wedding band of gold easily seen, his chin shadowed by the stubble of a day's growth of beard.

As if he knew that she watched him, his eyes opened. Sleepily at first and then with great alarm.

'Lilly?' His word was loud, quick, the sound of desperate horror and then relief when she blinked. 'I thought you were…'

He did not finish the sentence, but she knew exactly what he meant.

'I'm that ill?'

'No.' He leant forward now, the bulk of his shape shading out the lamp behind him so that she could no longer really see his face.

'How long have I been asleep?'

He looked at his watch. 'Twelve hours.'

She wriggled her toes and her fingers and tried to lift her head.

'I was shot?

'The bullet passed through the flesh on your side. Another inch and…' He didn't finish.

'I found Daniel's name beneath that of your wife's…'

She closed her eyes tight, the tears she wanted to hold back squeezing past and running down her cheeks into her hair. 'You risked everything for revenge?'

The look on his face was strained and tired, guilt marking gold eyes as plain as day. Turning away as he hesitated, she burrowed into her pillow, not wishing to hear anything else that he might say.

Hope and Charity came with Mrs Wilson in the late morning, the steaming porridge and freshly made bread they brought whetting an appetite that she had thought might never return again.

She could eat, she could smile, she could hold the girls' hands and pretend to them that all the violence and horror of yesterday was quite an adventure.

She did not ask where her husband was or where her cousin was. She did not dwell on what had happened to the bodies of those who had come to Woodruff with Daniel, or that when Lucas had aimed he had not meant to merely wound. He was a soldier trained for other things!

What else he was she did not know, did not want to know. He had lied and lied and lied and even for the time she had lain with him soft in the daylight with all the hours in the world to tell the truth, still he had not.

A dangerous man, a stranger, a husband who had risked his home for something that she didn't understand. She would not forgive him this. Ever.

She unclenched her fist as she saw Charity looking at her whitened knuckles and smiled.

She had to leave this place now, even with her side aching and the tiredness pulling her down.

'Would you both like to come with me today to see my house? My room has many toys that you might enjoy.'

The children's governess frowned deeply, but kept her counsel and for that at least Lilly was grateful.

The girls' quick smiles and nodding heads were much easier to deal with.

They reached Fairley Manor by lunchtime and her father was waiting for the coach with her aunt even as it came to a halt.

'Lillian.' He folded her in his arms and held her there, his familiar strength and honesty a buffer against all that had transpired.

After a moment she pulled away and introduced the girls, pleased when her father asked one of the servants to take the children to the kitchens and give them a 'treat'.

In his library he closed the door and helped her to a seat. When Lillian caught her reflection in the mirror, she was astonished by her paleness and could see why her father looked as worried as he did.

Pride stopped her saying anything. Ridiculous pride, if the truth be known, given that the story must be all over the countryside by now, though her father did not seem to have heard the gossip. For that she was glad.

'Can we stay here, Father?' she ventured instead and the line of worry on his brow deepened.

'For tonight?' He seemed to be testing the waters.

'For for ever,' she returned and burst into copious tears.

She felt better after a brandy and a Christmas tart, the seasonal joy having its own way of dulling her problems.

'I should never have forced you into this marriage— there has been nothing but problems ever since. In my defence I might add that Lucas Clairmont charmed me.'

She smiled. Her first smile since lying in bed with her husband clad in nothing save air. She shook away the thought.

'Then we are alike in that,' she returned.

'Perhaps if we filed for divorce to the Doctor's Commons under the name of insanity, and then went to the House of Lords with a suit? Though then, of course, we would need an Act of Parliament to enable you to ever marry again.'

Lillian frowned. Goodness, to get into a marriage was so easy, but to get out of one…?

She could not think of it, not now. She needed to get stronger first and build up her courage.

Reaching over, she took her father's fingers in her own. Sorrow filled her, for him, for them and for a future so uncertain now.

'Are the children his?'

'No. He is their guardian. They are his wife's sister's girls.'

'Yet you brought them here? Does he know that you have?'

She shook her head. 'I did not speak to him about it, but they need a home without violence. They need to be loved and cherished and protected. I can do that.'

Her father smiled. 'I believe that you can, my daughter. Welcome home.'

Lillian watched the driveway religiously all that evening and all the next day, but Lucas did not come. Nor did Daniel. She wondered if she should say something of her cousin's part in the whole fiasco to her aunt and then decided against it, for what exactly could she say?

Your son is a murderer just like my husband.

Christmas was now four days off and the house was dressed in its joyous coat for the children's sake as Hope and Charity dashed from this tree to that one, oblivious to every adult nuance that passed above their heads, the delight of wrapping presents and setting out gingerbread men and marzipan candies a wonderful game. Twinkling lights now hung on fragrant boughs and garlands of fresh sprigged pine bedecked the mantel, the children's hand in everything.

And then finally Lucas came at dusk on the second evening.

She met him on the front steps, glad that her father had gone with his manager to look at some problem on the property, for at least she did not have to worry about his reactions.

Gesturing for her husband to accompany her upstairs,

she took him to her bedroom, the intimacy of it affording her no problem with her state of mind.

'You lied about everything?'

He had the grace to look disconcerted. 'I did not tell you everything because I didn't want you involved—'

She stopped him, jumping in with such a shout the back of her throat hurt. 'Involved? When I am watching Lord Hawkhurst lying in a pool of blood whilst you shoot at my cousin like some wild-west gun-toting cowboy. And what of Hope and Charity? Two little girls exposed to fighting and shouting. I should not worry about that, I should not be involved?'

Pain crossed his face. 'Are the girls well?'

When Lillian nodded he looked so relieved that the anger she felt inside her was squashed down a little.

'I cannot even begin to understand a motive that would bring a man from America to England with the express purpose of killing another.'

'My wife had an affair with your cousin. I think that the child she carried was his.'

'Child?' The question spluttered to nothing on her lips.

Stopping, Lillian saw his heartbeat gather pace in the tender flesh at his neck.

'If he had been sorry I might have understood, could have forgiven. But he wasn't.'

He swiped his fingers through his hair.

'I was a soldier once.'

Lillian wondered as to his hesitancy in telling her of his involvement in a profession that was after all a noble one.

'I was seconded into intelligence work in my third year and I learned and did things that were not in any army rulebook. Once you know how to kill a man and do, you cross over a line. Whether or not it is for king and country you cross a line and you never come back from it. From that moment you are different...isolated, and the choices that are easy for every other person are not quite so for you.'

'You killed others in America?' The horror in his voice told her that he had.

'Not for fun or gain or glory. Not for that, you understand, but I have killed people. People who died because they believed in things that the military did not and sometimes they were good people...' He stopped again.

'Did you kill Daniel at Woodruff?'

'No.' She felt the relief at this denial until he continued, the world around her condensed into breath and heartbeat and pure raw fear!

'I wanted to, though. I came here to do just that, but found that I could not. When my uncle died, your cousin's name was the last thing on his lips. He had swindled him out of some land, you see, and made a fortune out of Stuart's infirmity. Paget had a hand in the bargain, too.'

'So when you mentioned the subject that night at the dinner table...'

'He knew that I knew.'

Vengeance. Retribution. Reprisal. The words shimmered in the air between them, harsh words actioned by a hardened man, used to blood and danger. A life for a life… She waited as he went on.

'The strangest thing about all of this is that it was not revenge in the end that saved me, Lillian. It was you.'

'Me?'

'I was married once to a woman who could not be happy, not with me, not with life, not with anything. The night she died her child was trying to be born…' The tremor in his voice was steadied by pure will-power. 'She would not stay at the house for she believed the midwife couldn't be trusted.'

'So you took her with you?'

'And overturned the carriage when she opened the door and threatened to jump out while shouting out the name of your cousin. I did not know exactly what that meant at the time, though now of course…' He shook his head. 'She died as I reached her.'

'My goodness! Were you hurt?'

'This scar…' His fingers traced the mark from his ear down to his collarbone. No slight injuries for him either, then, and a wife and child lost in betrayal.

'When I recovered and got back to the farm, I began to drink heavily. To forget.'

Water! She had never seen him touch anything stronger. The small pieces of a puzzle clicking into place. An explanation of what made a man complex. No easy choices. No one reason.

The truth. Not laundered. Not tampered with. Not

piecemeal. There was beauty in a man who did not try to hide behind illusion.

The silence stretched, boundless, and it was Lucas who broke it first.

'When I saw you at the Lenningtons' you were… perfect. Perfect in a way that I was not, had never been.'

'Perfect?' She shook her head. 'No one can be that.'

'Can they not?' His eyes were softer now, not as glitter-sharp as they had been, the anger in them dimmed by honesty and relief. 'There is a cherub on the chapel ceiling at my home with eyes and hair just your colour. Beside it is a sinner who is being…saved, I would guess, saved as you have saved me!'

There was violence in his words, desperation in the way his fingers reached out to the bare flesh of her arm.

'I am not a bad man, Lilly, and I need you. Need you beside me to make sense of the world and to shape my own.'

He tipped her chin up so that her eyes met his, direct and hard, no denial in the movement, no gentle easy ask.

'I would never hurt you, Lillian. Never. I would only ever love you.'

The words were not soft either, tumbling from nothing into everything.

Love.

You.

Overwhelming need and fear mixed with waiting.

Only them in this fire-filled cold winter's evening, three nights before Christmas, bound in troth for ever, the silence of the house wrapped around them.

Waiting for just one movement.

Towards him.

She simply stepped into his arms, her tears wetting the front of his jacket, the buttons old and mismatched and the elbows patched with leather.

He was perfect for her, too.

They stood there for a long time, listening to the heartbeats between them and feeling the warmth, not daring to move towards the bed for fear her father would knock on the door and find them. No, not wanting anything to be ruined again by violence and hostility.

Finally her father came, the sound of his steps in the passage and then a knock on the door. He came through quietly, waiting as they parted though their hands were still joined.

'I have been told what has happened.' His glance caught Lillian's. 'You are all right?'

'Yes.'

His face creased into a smile. 'And he has given you his secrets.'

'Not quite,' Luc said and his fingers tightened around her own. 'I am a wealthy man, Lilly. My estates are numerous in Virginia, for timber is a lucrative trade.'

'Wealthier than my father?'

'I am afraid so.'

'Then the flowers did not break you?'

'I beg your pardon?'

'Your bunch of flowers! I thought at the time they

must have cost you a small fortune so I saved one and dried it to show you.'

He shook his head. 'If you wanted a roomful, I could afford it.'

'But I don't,' she said solemnly and walked in to his waiting arms. 'All I want is you.'

The bells rang out from the village near Woodruff, tumbling Yuletide bells with joy on their edge, though they were muffled by the snow that had fallen all day, filling the windows with white and making ghosts of the trees in the garden.

They had eaten and danced and sang, and the sweet smells of cinnamon and spices hung in the air, the last of the visitors to Fairley finally gone and the big Bible in the front parlour closed from the many different readings. The whole day had been noisy and rushed and wonderful. None of the silent ease of Christmases past but all of a building excitement and joy, with the squeals of delight of Hope and Charity.

Goodness, she had changed completely in these few weeks, for she could not imagine again a pale and ordered Christmas, nor a home with as few guests as she had always cultivated.

Charity and Hope had made up games to play, Stephen had organised charades and Patrick had shadowed Lucas all day with questions of Virginia and its riches.

Her father had spent a quiet moment with her in the

early afternoon, taking her aside to give her his present, the pearls that she knew had been her mother's.

'She was a person who made one wrong choice, Lillian. But before that she had made many right ones. You, for instance,' he said and kissed the tip of her nose.

It was the first time she had heard him talk of Rebecca since her death, and that gift was as important to her as the double strand of matched pearls that were strong in her memory.

'You told me once, Father, that I would thank you for this marriage and I do.'

'Lucas has let Daniel leave the country, so his stupidity shall not be the ruin of the Davenport name after all. I think even Jean understands the generosity of Lucas's gesture and has elected to go along with Daniel.'

She smiled at her father's relief, the burden of the family reputation one he had always taken so very diligently to heart.

'You look better than you have in a long while, Father.'

He smiled. 'I believe I am well because you are happy, my love.'

And much later when the moon hung high she smiled again as Lucas placed a kiss on her stomach where candlelight played across her skin.

'I want lots more children, Lilly. Sisters and brothers for Hope and Charity.'

The ruby caught in the light as she brushed the length of his hair from his face.

'I wanted to ask you about the inscription inside the ring.'

'I had it engraved in London for you.'

'But you did not know then that I would even marry you!'

' "*Whither thou goest, I will go.*" I knew that after our first kiss in your drawing room.'

'It was always just us then?'

'Just us,' he whispered back and, bringing a sprig of mistletoe from the cabinet beside the bed, held it above them, a wicked smile in his dancing amber eyes.

Bestselling author Lynne Graham is back with a fabulous new trilogy!

PREGNANT BRIDES

Three ordinary girls—naive, but also honest and plucky…

Three fabulously wealthy, impossibly handsome and very ruthless men…

When opposites attract and passion leads to pregnancy… it can only mean marriage!

Available next month from Harlequin Presents®: the first installment

DESERT PRINCE, BRIDE OF INNOCENCE

* * *

'THIS EVENING I'm flying to New York for two weeks,' Jasim imparted with a casualness that made her heart sink like a stone. 'That's why I had you brought here. I own this apartment and you'll be comfortable here while I'm abroad.'

'I can afford my own accommodation although I may not need it for long. I'll have another job by the time you get back—'

Jasim released a slightly harsh laugh. 'There's no need for you to look for another position. How would I ever see you? Don't you understand what I'm offering you?'

Elinor stood very still. 'No, I must be incredibly thick because I haven't quite worked out yet what you're offering me….'

His charismatic smile slashed his lean dark visage. 'Naturally, I want to take care of you….'

HPEX0110A

'No, thanks.' Elinor forced a smile and mentally willed him not to demean her with some sordid proposition. 'The only man who will ever take *care* of me with my agreement will be my husband. I'm willing to wait for you to come back but I'm not willing to be kept by you. I'm a very independent woman and what I give, I give freely.'

Jasim frowned. 'You make it all sound so serious.'

'What happened between us last night left pure chaos in its wake. Right now, I don't know whether I'm on my head or my heels. I'll stay for a while because I have nowhere else to go in the short term. So maybe it's good that you'll be away for a while.'

Jasim pulled out his wallet to extract a card. 'My private number,' he told her, presenting her with it as though it was a precious gift, which indeed it was. Many women would have done just about anything to gain access to that direct hotline to him, but his staff guarded his privacy with scrupulous care.

Before he could close the wallet, his blood ran cold in his veins. How could he have made such a serious oversight? What if he had got her pregnant? He knew that an unplanned pregnancy would engulf his life like an avalanche, crush his freedom and suffocate him. He barely stilled a shudder at the threat of such an outcome and thought how ironic it was that what his older brother had longed and prayed for to secure the line to the throne should strike Jasim as an absolute disaster....

* * *

What will proud Prince Jasim do if Elinor is expecting his royal baby? Perhaps an arranged marriage is the only solution! But will Elinor agree? Find out in DESERT PRINCE, BRIDE OF INNOCENCE by Lynne Graham [#2884], available from Harlequin Presents® in January 2010.

AT HIS
Service

From glass slippers to silk sheets

Once upon a time there was a humble housekeeper.
Proud but poor, she went to work for a charming and
ruthless rich man!

She thought her place was below stairs—
but her gorgeous boss had other ideas.

Her place was in the bedroom, between his
luxurious silk sheets.

Stripped of her threadbare uniform, buxom and blushing
in his bed, she'll discover that a woman's work has never
been so much fun!

Look out for:

POWERFUL ITALIAN,
PENNILESS HOUSEKEEPER
by India Grey
#2886

Available January 2010

REQUEST YOUR
FREE BOOKS!

Harlequin® Historical
Historical Romantic Adventure!

2 FREE NOVELS PLUS 2 FREE GIFTS!

YES! Please send me 2 FREE Harlequin® Historical novels and my 2 FREE gifts (gifts are worth about $10). After receiving them, if I don't wish to receive any more books, I can return the shipping statement marked "cancel". If I don't cancel, I will receive 6 brand-new novels every month and be billed just $4.94 per book in the U.S. or $5.49 per book in Canada. That's a savings of 20% off the cover price! It's quite a bargain! Shipping and handling is just 50¢ per book.* I understand that accepting the 2 free books and gifts places me under no obligation to buy anything. I can always return a shipment and cancel at any time. Even if I never buy another book, the two free books and gifts are mine to keep forever.

246 HDN EYS3   349 HDN EYTF

Name _____ (PLEASE PRINT) _____

Address _____ Apt. # _____

City _____ State/Prov. _____ Zip/Postal Code _____

Signature (if under 18, a parent or guardian must sign)

Mail to the **Harlequin Reader Service:**
IN U.S.A.: P.O. Box 1867, Buffalo, NY 14240-1867
IN CANADA: P.O. Box 609, Fort Erie, Ontario L2A 5X3

Not valid to current subscribers of Harlequin Historical books.

Want to try two free books from another line?
Call 1-800-873-8635 or visit www.morefreebooks.com.

* Terms and prices subject to change without notice. Prices do not include applicable taxes. Sales tax applicable in N.Y. Canadian residents will be charged applicable provincial taxes and GST. Offer not valid in Quebec. This offer is limited to one order per household. All orders subject to approval. Credit or debit balances in a customer's account(s) may be offset by any other outstanding balance owed by or to the customer. Please allow 4 to 6 weeks for delivery. Offer available while quantities last.

Your Privacy: Harlequin Books is committed to protecting your privacy. Our Privacy Policy is available online at www.eHarlequin.com or upon request from the Reader Service. From time to time we make our lists of customers available to reputable third parties who may have a product or service of interest to you. If you would prefer we not share your name and address, please check here. ☐

HH09R

COMING NEXT MONTH FROM

HARLEQUIN®
HISTORICAL

Available December 29, 2009

- **THE ROGUE'S DISGRACED LADY**
by **Carole Mortimer**
(Regency)
Society gossip has kept Lady Juliet Boyd out of the public eye: all
she really wants is a quiet life. Finally persuaded to accept a summer
house-party invitation, she meets the scandalous Sebastian St. Claire,
a man who makes her feel things, want things, *need* things she's never
experienced before.... But does Sebastian really want Juliet—or just the
truth behind her disgrace?

- **THE KANSAS LAWMAN'S PROPOSAL**
by **Carol Finch**
(Western)
Falling in love with dashing lawman Nathan Montgomery was not the
outcome Rachel expected when she joined a Kansas medicine show
wagon! But Dodge City is no place for a single young seamstress, and
despite the secrets that Nate and Rachel hide, they soon begin to need
each other's comfort and protection far more than they anticipated....

- **THE EARL AND THE GOVERNESS**
by **Sarah Elliott**
(Regency)
Impoverished, alone and on the run, Isabelle Thomas desperately needs
the governess position William Stanton, Earl of Lennox, offers her. But
when their passion explodes in a bone-melting kiss, Isabelle knows she
must leave—only the earl has other plans for his innocent governess....

- **PREGNANT BY THE WARRIOR**
by **Denise Lynn**
(Medieval)
Lea of Montreau must marry and produce an heir, or lose her lands. The
headstrong and beautiful lady plots to seduce a particular stranger to
produce an heir—but the stranger is none other than ruggedly handsome
Jared of Warehaven—her onetime betrothed childhood sweetheart! Lea
previously rejected Jared, and now he wants his revenge—by marriage!